Time of Reckoning

Ry Tyler is in no doubt; he has recently seen his old friend
Slim Freeman alive and kicking. So how come Freeman's
grave is on Boot Hill?

Tyler's search for the truth leads him into a world of
intrigue and danger, where nothing is as it seems. What about
the marshal and his deputy? What about Sadie Roundtree
and the oldster, Diamondback Casey? Can he count on
anybody? And that's before the notorious Lassiter gang
arrives in town. Are they involved somehow? Does the island
in the middle of Green Fork River with its decaying riverboat
wreck hold a clue to the answers?

Tyler must follow a long trail till he arrives at the final time
of reckoning.

Time of Reckoning

Colin Bainbridge

A Black Horse Western

ROBERT HALE

ISBN 978-0-7198-2935-2

The Crowood Press
The Stable Block
Crowood Lane
Ramsbury
Marlborough
Wiltshire SN8 2HR

www.bhwesterns.com

Robert Hale is an imprint
of The Crowood Press

Typeset by
Derek Doyle & Associates, Shaw Heath
Printed and bound in Great Britain by
4Bind Ltd, Stevenage, SG1 2XT

CHAPTER ONE

Ry Tyler paused for a moment to take in a deep draught of the cool night air before stepping through the batwing doors of the Spur Saloon. The atmosphere inside was heavy and fetid. He pushed his way to the bar and placed a foot on the rail.

'What'll it be?'

'Whiskey.'

The bartender poured, giving him a searching glance as he did so.

'Passin' through?' he asked.

'That depends.'

'Depends on what?'

'On whether I get some answers to a few questions.'

The barman looked at him more closely.

'You'll need to check in those guns,' he said.

Tyler tossed down the whiskey.

'Pour me another,' he said.

As the barman poured, Tyler's eyes searched the

room through the mirror. The place was crowded and the tone was raucous. A piano began to play.

'Is it always as busy as this?' Tyler asked.

'Not always. A bunch of cowboys hit town. Guess they're takin' a break. The trail north passes close by.'

'Thought I could smell cattle as I came in,' Tyler replied.

The bartender moved away to tend some other customers, but was soon back again.

'Those questions you mentioned,' he said. 'Maybe I could try answerin' a few.'

Tyler nodded.

'Sure. Maybe you can help.'

'I've been around a long time,' the barman replied. 'There ain't much goin' on I don't get to know about.'

Tyler looked at him long and hard.

'Then perhaps you can tell me why there's a grave marked Slim Freeman up on the hill when I saw him just the day before yesterday.'

It seemed to Tyler that the barman held his gaze for just the fraction of a second too long.

'You must have been mistaken,' he replied. 'Slim Freeman's been dead and buried a good four months or more now. Or maybe you're thinkin' of someone else.'

'You know the name?'

'Sure. Slim used to come in here now and then. Not regularly. He tended to keep himself to himself.'

'What do you know about him?'

'Not much. Like I say, he kept himself to himself.'

'Did he have any friends?'

The barman shrugged.

'Not that I know of. Really, I can't tell you much more.'

'Where'd he live?'

'He had a place on Chestnut Street, just opposite the Magnolia.'

The barman stopped and turned his head. A woman had approached; Tyler had seen her through the mirror. She was hard to miss.

'Did I hear mention of the Magnolia?' she said.

The barman looked confused but she didn't give him time to reply. Instead she turned to Tyler.

'Let me introduce myself,' she said. 'I'm Sadie Roundtree. I run this place and the Magnolia too.'

Tyler exchanged a brief glance with the barman before turning to the newcomer.

'Pleased to meet you, ma'am,' he replied. 'I'm Tyler, Ry Tyler.'

'Ry Tyler,' she mused. 'I have a feeling I might have heard that name before.'

'I doubt it. I'm new to these parts.'

'I get around,' she replied.

Tyler took note of her rounded figure and yellow hair which was piled on top of her head.

'I guess you do,' he said.

'What I mean is that I haven't always lived in Green Fork. Not that I have anything against it. It's a nice town. Peaceful. We kind of like it that way.' She paused. 'Mr Conway mentioned the Magnolia. Do I take it that means you might be looking for a place to stay?'

'I wasn't thinking of it,' Tyler replied.

She took a few seconds to think.

'Why don't you and I take a seat and talk it over?' she said.

Without giving him a chance to reply, she quickly turned to the barman.

'Bring the rest of that bottle over to my table,' she said, 'and an extra tumbler.'

'Yes, ma'am.'

She turned and glided away and with a final glance at the barman, Tyler picked up his glass and followed her to a corner table which he guessed was reserved for her. She halted and he pulled out her chair. She sat down and he took a seat opposite.

'I don't see that we have anything to talk about,' he said, attempting to take the initiative.

'You're sitting next to me all the same,' she replied. She poured the whiskey.

'I take it you haven't met with Marshal Dick?' she said.

The question was unexpected and it took him a moment to adjust.

'As a matter of fact I haven't,' he replied. 'Is there any reason I should?'

She glanced at his holsters.

'You might have noticed no one else is carrying

8

firearms. That's the marshal's doing. Anyone arriving in town has to check them in.'

'It's funny,' Tyler replied, 'but the barman told me almost the same thing.'

'Just reminding you then. It might be a good idea for you to go along and make his acquaintance.'

'Sure. I'll put it at the top of my agenda. And by the way, if you were considering offering me a room at the Magnolia, I'm already booked in at the Franconia Hotel. Not that I don't appreciate it.'

'The Franconia is a whole lot more expensive.'

'When I run low, I'll get back to you.'

'You might just do that, but the offer might not hold.'

Tyler took a swig of whiskey. The hubbub had grown louder and they had to lean closer to make themselves heard.

'Do I take it you will be staying in town for a while?' Sadie said.

'Just as long as it takes.'

'To do what?'

Tyler thought for a moment.

'To find Slim Freeman.'

He watched closely for any sign of a reaction but there was none.

'Slim Freeman? If it's the same person, Slim Freeman is dead. His grave is up on Boot Hill.'

'I know. I've seen it. The only problem with that is that I saw him only recently.'

'You couldn't have. You must have been mistaken.'

9

'I don't think so.'

'And why are you so keen to find this man?'

'He was a friend of mine. I ain't seen him in a long time. Then, like I say, I saw him, right here in town.'

'At least you think you did. If you haven't seen him in a long time, he might have changed.'

'It was him. He was walking by on the far side of the street, a little way down. By the time I'd crossed, he was gone.'

'So what were you doing up on Boot Hill? Do you make a practice of visiting graveyards?'

'I was walking along the levee and cut through to get back to town. It was pure chance I saw the head-stone.'

The headstone had been in quite a prominent place; was there something significant in that? Sadie didn't reply and he took another sip of the whiskey before speaking again.

'If you don't mind me saying so, you seem to be taking quite an interest in what I'm doing.'

She laughed.

'Not at all,' she replied. 'Just being neighbourly. After all, you're a stranger in town.'

He leaned back in his chair to observe the scene.

'There are quite a few strangers in town,' he replied. 'You don't appear to be quite so interested in them.'

Again she laughed.

'They're just cowboys,' she replied. 'By tomorrow they'll be back on the trail. In the meantime, they're welcome just so long as they spend their cash and don't cause any trouble.'

'They're rowdy.'

'That's fine, nothing I can't deal with. If they were to get out of hand, the marshal can step in.'

'You seem to hold the marshal in high regard.'

For a moment he thought he thought he detected a flicker of animation pass across her features.

'The marshal is a good man. He's brought law and order to this town. The townsfolk owe him a lot.'

He finished the last of the whiskey and got to his feet.

'I guess I'll see for myself tomorrow,' he said.

She looked puzzled.

'Didn't you advise me to hand in my guns?' he added.

Without waiting for a reply, he turned aside and made his way to the batwings. He pushed them open and when he stepped outside, the cool night air hit him like a douche of cold water. He stood by the rail, breathing it in before turning away and bending his steps in the direction of the river. The street was deserted. As he passed on his way, he noticed a light in the marshal's office and for a moment was tempted to pay him a visit right then and there. However, after a moment's hesitation, he continued on his way.

By the river the air was fresher and set the leaves rustling. A thin mist hung low over the water. Downstream, the river was divided by an islet which loomed against the darkening skyline. He stood by the edge of the wharf and lit a cigarette, thinking all the while about what had just transpired in the saloon. The woman had not tried to evade his questions, but he had a feeling that she wasn't being quite open with him. There was something ambiguous in her manner. It seemed to him he might have done better with the barman. In fact, now he reflected on the matter, it was almost as if she had deliberately interrupted his conversation with the barman. Why would she do that? Was she afraid in some way that he might give too much away? One question he should certainly have asked, and that was how Slim Freeman had died. But then he was sure he had seen Freeman, so he couldn't be dead. It might have been interesting to hear their version of the so-called cause of death. If he asked around, maybe he would find discrepancies in the various accounts.

He had almost finished his smoke when he suddenly tensed. He was sure he had heard something. Dropping the cigarette into the river, he turned to glance behind him. The wharf was backed by some run-down warehouses and for an instant he thought he detected a sign of movement. Quickly stepping away from his exposed spot into a more shadowy corner, he began to work his way round towards the back of the wharf. His ears were strained to catch any further sounds, but he could detect nothing. He had about decided that he had been mistaken when the silence of the evening was shattered by the wail of a cat quickly followed by the sound of something crashing to the ground. Tyler drew his gun and sprang forward and as he did so, a dim form disentangled itself from the shadows and came forward with its hands in the air.

'Don't shoot!' a voice called.

The man was hobbling and it was clear that he had injured his leg in the fall. 'I don't mean to cause any trouble.'

The man came to a halt. Tyler could see that he was an oldster. His straggling hair was white and his left eye gleamed strangely in the darkness.

'What were you doin' skulking back there?' Tyler said.

'Lookin' for you. I saw you leave the saloon but then I lost you. I figured—'

'So you were back there in the saloon?' Tyler interrupted.

'Sure. I work there, leastways some of the time. I'm the swamper.'

Tyler put away his gun and came up to the oldster. When he was close, he could see that his eye gleamed because it was made of glass.

'That durn cat,' the man said. 'It got between my feet and tripped me up. Look, I've split my trousers.'

Tyler glanced down. The man's trousers were ripped at the knee and blood was oozing from a cut. He looked so dejected that Tyler couldn't help laughing.

'Here,' he said, taking out his pack of Bull

Durham and offering it to the oldster. The old man rolled himself a cigarette and handed it back to Tyler before lighting up.

'Thanks,' he said. He looked about.

'Mind if I take a seat on that old cask I knocked over?' he said.

'Might be a good idea,' Tyler replied.

He turned the cask upright and the oldster half sat and half leaned against it. He inhaled deeply.

'That's better,' he said.

'Let me take a look at that knee.'

Tyler examined the wound. It was quite deep but not serious. Taking his bandanna, he wrapped it around the knee.

'You'll survive,' he said. 'But you were taking a risk. You're lucky you didn't get shot.'

They were silent for a time while the oldster enjoyed his cigarette before Tyler spoke again.

'You said you were lookin' for me. I figure you'd better explain why.'

The oldster inhaled deeply and then blew out a couple of smoke rings before replying.

'I couldn't help overhearing what you had to say back at the saloon,' he said.

'What, you were listening in to my conversation with Miss Roundtree?'

The man nodded.

'You couldn't have overheard what we were sayin'. You must have been listenin' deliberately.'

'Accidentally, deliberately, what does it matter?

The upshot is the same. You're lookin' for Slim Freeman. I know where you can find him.'

Tyler was completely taken aback. It took him a moment or two to register what the oldster had just said.

'You know where he is?' he repeated.

'Yup. If you like, I can take you there.'

'I got the impression that folks seemed to think Slim Freeman is dead. Both Miss Roundtree and the barman told me that.'

'It ain't true. He's as alive as I am.'

Tyler looked the oldster up and down.

'That ain't sayin' much,' he replied.

'Listen,' the oldster said. 'Meet me at the livery stables after sunup. I ain't got a horse, so you'll have to hire me one.'

'Why would I do that?'

'You're lookin' for Freeman. I'll take you to where he's hidin' out.'

'Hidin' out? Who's he hidin' from?'

The oldster gave him a sly look.

'I figured you might know that,' he replied.

Tyler thought for a few moments. He was feeling confused and not a little disorientated, but he didn't have any better plan than to go along with the oldster's suggestion.

'If we're gonna be ridin' together,' he said, 'you'd better tell me your name.'

'Diamondback Casey,' the oldster replied.

'Diamondback?'

'That's what folks call me. I guess I've kind of got used to it.'

'But why Diamondback?'

The oldster shrugged.

'I don't know. I guess it's cos I'm kinda scaly. Like a snake.'

Tyler gave him another look.

'Don't worry. There ain't nothin' wrong with me, apart from bein' old.'

Tyler was thoughtful again.

'What about that grave on Boot Hill?' he said. 'It had Slim Freeman's name on it.'

Casey shrugged.

'There's a body buried there,' he said. 'But it ain't Slim Freeman's.'

'How do you know that?'

'Because as well as doin' some work swampin' at the saloon, I help out now and then at the undertakers.'

Tyler gave him a searching look.

'What do you get out of this?' he asked.

The oldster scratched his chin.

'So far,' he said, 'a smoke and a horse. That's not a bad start.'

Tyler laughed.

'Here,' he said, holding out the pack of Bull Durham. 'Take it. You're doin' better than you thought.'

The oldster seized it.

'I'll see you tomorrow,' he said. He began to limp away.

'Are you sure that leg is OK?' Tyler called after him.

The oldster replied with a gesture. Tyler watched as he disappeared into the shadows before eventually making his own way back into town.

Soon after Tyler had left the saloon and she was satisfied he was gone, Sadie Roundtree made her own exit from the saloon and walked over to the marshal's office. A light was still burning and after knocking on the door, she opened it and made her way inside.

'Sadie!' he exclaimed, with more of an air of pleasure than surprise at seeing her.

He was sitting at a bare table on which stood a bottle of bourbon, but on her sudden appearance he quickly got to his feet and embraced her, after which he made his way to a corner cabinet, and got out an extra glass.

'Join me?' he said. 'It's maybe not quite what you're accustomed to, but it isn't half bad.'

'Yes, that would be nice,' she replied. When he came over with the glass, she placed herself on a chair to the side of the table while he poured.

'Well,' he said, handing her the glass, 'I didn't expect to see you till later. I guess there's some reason you're here.'

She took a sip.

'There's a reason. A good reason.'

He looked at her and his expression changed.

17

'Just now there was a feller in the saloon askin' about Freeman.'

The marshal sat upright.

'What feller?' he asked.

'I've not seen him before. He's new in town. He said his name was Ry Tyler. I gather he's stayin' at the Franconia.'

'So what's his connection with Freeman?'

Sadie shrugged her bare shoulders.

'I don't know. But he obviously knows Freeman. He said he recognized him when he saw him recently.'

'You told him he must have got it wrong? That Freeman is dead?'

'Of course I did. But I don't think he believes it.'

'How old is this *hombre*?'

'About my age. Or Freeman's.'

The marshal muttered something under his breath.

'What do you think?' he asked. 'How much do you figure he knows?'

'Your guess is as good as mine. But if Freeman's right about the Lassiter boys bein' out again, it would fit.'

The marshal considered her words.

'It might just be a coincidence,' he said.

'You don't really believe that? Too much of a coincidence, I'd say. At least, I think we need to work on that assumption.'

'Work? What do you mean, work?'

'I mean we'd better be prepared. You especially.'

The marshal reflected for a moment.

'I think I'll stop by and pay this Tyler a visit tomorrow. See if I can find out a bit more about him.' His brow furrowed. 'If you're right about this, and it's not just a coincidence, he might not be the only one to show up.'

There was a pause. Both of them were deep in thought. Presently the marshal reached for the bottle and topped up their glasses again.

'Leave it to me for now,' he said.

'Are you still coming over later?'

The marshal's face creased in a grin.

'You betcha,' he replied.

She laughed.

'You're makin' an assumption. Maybe I'm not available. Maybe I need some time to myself.'

He got up and, leaning over her chair, placed his hands over her breasts.

'Then why ask?' he said.

She turned her face up towards him and he bent down to kiss her before moving away. She got slowly to her feet.

'Don't frighten the customers by flashing that tin star,' she said.

When he got back to the hotel, Tyler sensed that something was wrong. There was nothing definite, but his instincts rarely lied. He stood for a moment outside his room, listening intently, but he could hear nothing. He drew his six-gun and, holding it steady, inserted the key into the lock with his other hand. He turned it slowly and when the door was unlocked, he suddenly kicked it open and rushed inside. At first he couldn't see anything except the play of some lights across one wall. Gradually his eyes adjusted to the dark. The room was empty but he still had a feeling that not everything was as it should be. He crouched low, still alert for any indication that somebody might be there, and only when he was completely satisfied that he was alone did he place the gun back in its holster and light the lamp.

Immediately he saw that one drawer of the bureau by his bedside was partially open. He was pretty sure that he had left it closed. He pulled it open and looked closely inside, even though he knew it was empty. Evidently, unless his memory was playing him false in that regard, somebody had entered his room and rummaged through the bureau. He quickly checked for other signs of disturbance but could find none. Whoever it was must have used a key. Did that mean it was somebody connected with the hotel? It looked that way. On the other hand, the keys to all the rooms were simply left hanging on hooks behind the reception desk. Anybody could have taken one while the receptionist was absent. In fact, the desk clerk had not been at his post when he came through the lobby. He was about to go down the stairs to confront him, assuming he was back at his post, but a moment's reflection was enough for him to realize he was being silly. He had the key. He had just opened the door with it. He needed to get a grip on himself. There could of course be another spare key. Another door opened on to a balcony; the intruder might have got in that way. Quickly he crossed the room and stepped outside. There was no obvious sign of a disturbance but when he bent down to examine the wooden platform, his keen eyes made out the unmistakable impression of boots in the dust. Taking the lamp, he had a closer look. One impression was particularly discernible. It was right by the rail and it was a fair bet it was made by someone climbing over. He looked down at the street below. He was on the second floor and the drop wasn't particularly high. What was more, the print of the boot made a distinctive mark. It wasn't much to go on, but for a man who lived by his wits, it could be a valuable clue. Confident that he had worked out how the intruder had entered his room, he looked up.

The street was deserted. Only the lights from the saloon still spilled out on to the main drag. Was Diamondback there now? Or did he stay somewhere else? He had a sudden thought. Had the oldster been sent to keep him occupied while somebody inspected his room? Could it have been Sadie Roundtree or one of her acolytes? The bartender perhaps? If not, who else could it have been? And what were they hoping to find? Sadie had mentioned Marshal Dick. He might have an interest in checking on any strangers new in town. But if it was him, he

21

had gone about things in an odd fashion. Suddenly he was distracted by a loud outburst of noise coming from the saloon. Moments later the batwings sprung open and a bunch of men burst through. They were shouting and laughing as they made their way to their horses tied to the hitch-rack. Tyler's guess was that they were some of the trail hands Sadie had mentioned. Still whooping, they climbed into leather and then took off down the street in a cloud of dust.

CHAPTER TWO

The next morning, after he had eaten, Tyler made his way to the livery where he had already stabled his sorrel. Given the ambiguities of the situation, he had slept remarkably well and was feeling ready for what the day might bring. He half expected Diamondback not to turn up. The arrangements had been somewhat vague, but when he reached the stables the oldster was there. In fact, he seemed to have made himself at home and was in conversation with another older man whom Tyler guessed was the ostler. He looked up at Tyler's approach.

'Howdy!' he said.

'Howdy.'

The ostler gave Tyler a suspicious glance.

'I've picked me a hoss,' Diamondback said. 'In fact, she's all saddled up and ready to go.'

'Yours too,' the ostler said to Tyler.

'That's fine,' Tyler said. 'How much do I owe you?'

He paid over the money and they all walked to the

back of the stables. He hadn't paid a lot and when he saw the horse he could see why.

'OK,' he said to Diamondback. 'Now that's settled, let's get goin'.'

They led their horses out of the back of the stables where they mounted.

'See you later, Bart,' Diamondback said to the ostler.

The man nodded as they touched their spurs to the horses' flanks and set off down the street. It ran parallel to the main drag but was not much more than a back street. For some reason, Tyler felt quite glad that no-one saw them leave. In a matter of moments they had left the town behind.

'Which way are we headed?' Tyler said.

By way of reply Diamondback waved his hand in front of him, pointing with his index finger. It seemed a little vague, but Tyler didn't press him further. Instead, he contented himself with taking note of the country they were riding through. It was river country, flat with scattered clumps of trees, but after a time the ground rose as they began to climb away from the river valley. A line of low hills appeared ahead of them and when they reached the crest of the slope they saw, way off beneath them, a long line of cattle.

'They're headed up from the Gulf country,' Diamondback said. 'They've got a long way to go.'

'Some of the boys from the outfit were in the saloon last night,' Tyler remarked.

'Yeah. The trail passes close by. It's brought a lot of trade but a peck of trouble too. Keeps the marshal on his toes.'

They veered away, dropping below the skyline and riding along another stretch of hills till they dipped down again and followed the course of a stream running through a narrow valley. Presently Diamondback brought his horse to a stop and pointed ahead of them to a clump of vegetation backed by a wall of rock.

'That's where you'll find your man,' he said.

'What? You mean that's where Freeman is hanging out?'

'Yup. Take a peek through your glasses. There's a little disused shack.'

Tyler drew out his field-glasses and took a closer look. He soon picked out the cabin, partly hidden by trees and bushes. It looked to be in a bad state. He put the glasses back in their case and turned to Diamondback.

'You haven't said much about Freeman,' he said.

The oldster shrugged.

'I ain't one to pry,' he said. 'I guess if Freeman wants to lie low, he's got his reasons.'

'How long has he been here?'

'I don't know.'

'It ain't far from town. He must have stopped by for provisions or somethin'. That's how I came to spot him. He didn't seem to be takin' much effort to stay incognito.'

'Incog. . . .' Diamondback began.

'Never mind. I still don't get why he would go to the lengths of settin' up his own tombstone to make people think he was dead. Whoever he wanted to fool, it wasn't so much the townsfolk. It didn't fool you.'

Diamondback looked Tyler straight in the face.

'You ain't said what you're doin' here.'

Tyler thought for a moment.

'Call it chance,' he said.

Diamondback looked as if he was about to add something, but instead he just shook his head and spat.

'No point in sittin' here,' Tyler said. 'Let's go take a look.'

They rode on till they were close in the shelter of the trees when Tyler called a halt.

'That's as far as we go with these horses,' he said.

'What's the problem?'

'No problem. I just don't figure on takin' any chances.'

'Chances?'

'If Freeman chose to lie low, he ain't likely to be in a welcoming mood.'

Diamondback shrugged.

'I suppose you've got a point,' he said.

They dismounted and tied their horses before stepping out on foot. It didn't take long for them to catch sight of the cabin among the trees. Tyler regarded it closely. It showed no sign of being occupied.

Suddenly he felt apprehensive. He glanced at Diamondback. The oldster seemed to be up front, but how could he be sure he wasn't being set up? The whole thing could be a trap.

'Give me your gun,' he said.

Diamondback looked at him in surprise. The expression on his face seemed to be genuine.

'Sorry,' Tyler said. 'Just a precaution.'

Diamondback hesitated a moment before bringing out his gun and handing it to Tyler. Tyler looked at it. It was an old Navy model, .36 calibre. He tucked it into his belt.

'Stay close to me,' he said.

He crept forward, accompanied by the oldster, till they reached the side of the cabin. The window frame was empty and Tyler peered inside. The place was a ruin and covered in grime and dirt. A few items of furniture lay scattered about. Tyler moved away and started towards the front. What was left of the porch sagged and the door hung loosely on its hinges. Tyler peered within and then, telling Diamondback to stay where he was for the moment, rushed inside. There was only the one room. A filthy mattress lay in one corner and a rank smell pervaded the air. There was clearly no one about.

'OK!' he shouted. 'You can come on in.'

Diamondback's figure appeared in the doorway. There was a look of distaste on his features.

'Hell,' he said. 'A body would have to have a mighty good reason to want to stay here.'

'There's nobody around. The place hasn't been lived in for years. What made you think Freeman would be here?'

'I saw him ride out this way. I followed him. At the time, I thought he was dead.'

'You followed him all the way here?'

'Yeah.'

'What did he do? Did he enter the cabin?'

'He did, but I didn't stay around. I'd seen enough. I figured this was his hideout. I'd taken enough risks following him here.'

Tyler was thoughtful. 'Maybe he stayed here briefly, but I doubt it.'

'Sorry to have led you on a wild goose chase.'

Tyler was thoughtful for a few moments longer. Then he drew Diamondback's gun out of his belt and handed it back.

'No hard feelin's,' he said.

The oldster looked somewhat bemused, but Tyler's expression presented a strong contrast. He couldn't be sure, but he thought he had an inkling of what Freeman might have been doing out at the cabin. It was only a vague hint, but maybe things were beginning to make a little more sense.

Neither Tyler nor Diamondback had much to say as they rode back to town. Tyler was mulling over the events of the previous few days, and the oldster seemed to be embarrassed about the outcome of their visit to the shack. He was certainly crestfallen. Taking a look at him from time to time, Tyler couldn't help but grin at his forlorn appearance. As they approached the outskirts of town, he pulled his sorrel alongside the oldster's nag.

'It wasn't your fault Freeman wasn't there,' he said.

'I swear I followed him to the shack.'

'I don't doubt it. But by the look of the place, he can't have stayed long.'

The oldster's expression continued to be glum.

'If he's not there now,' Tyler said, 'he must be somewhere else. You know this area better than I do. I'd appreciate it if you keep your ear to the ground and let me know if you pick up any information.'

The oldster's expression immediately brightened. It was clear that he felt a need to be of use to somebody.

'Sure,' he said. 'I'll do that.'

They stopped off at the livery stables and left the horses in the care of the ostler.

'Remember what I said,' Tyler told Diamondback. 'But be discreet. I don't want everyone knowin' my business.'

'You can count on me,' Diamondback said.

Tyler watched his diminutive figure shuffle away down the street till he was distracted by a voice from behind him.

'The old feller seems to have taken a shine to you.'

Tyler turned. The voice was that of the ostler.

'Why do you say that?'

'He was talkin' about you.'

'Oh yeah, what did he say?'

'Oh, mainly that it was decent of you to patch him up some after he'd taken a fall. He showed me his leg. The knee was badly cut. I told him to visit the doc.'

'Good advice.'

'He's tough as an alligator's hide. He won't see any doctor.'

'How did he come by that eye?'

The ostler shrugged.

'I don't know, but you should get him to take it out and clean it some time. It's better than a vaudeville act.'

Tyler wasn't sure how to take that comment. Once he had settled with the ostler, he made his way back to the hotel. Outside his room, he stopped to listen but he didn't have the same presentiment that somebody had been there as previously. He opened the door and stepped inside. Unstrapping his gun belt, he placed it over the bed head before removing his boots and lying down on the mattress. After a short time he fell into a doze from which he was aroused by the sound of knocking. Immediately alert, he drew his gun from its holster and stepped over to the door.

'Who is it?' he called.

'Marshal Dick.'

He quickly placed the gun back in its holster and then opened the door for the marshal to step through.

He was older than Tyler had anticipated. His hair was streaked with grey and the lines around his eyes and mouth were sharply etched.

'Hope you don't mind me stoppin' by,' he said.

Tyler shook his head.

'Why should I mind? I'm just wonderin' to what I owe the courtesy.'

The marshal took a chair while Tyler sat on the edge of the bed.

'I believe you've met Sadie Roundtree. She and I are old friends. She probably mentioned my name. It's Dick, Harvey Dick.'

'You're right on both counts. I'm Ry Tyler.'

The marshal leaned forward and they shook hands.

'This is just a courtesy visit,' Dick said.

'Do you always call on newcomers to Green Fork?'

'Not always. Only if I feel it might be useful.'

The marshal looked around the room, his glance finally falling on Tyler's gun belt slung across the head-board.

'I guess you didn't see the notice as you rode into town,' he said.

'What notice?'

'The one that says the carryin' of firearms is strictly forbidden.'

'I guess not.'

'I'll overlook that one, just so long as you stop by and hand 'em over to my deputy before sundown.'

'Sure. Be glad to oblige.'

The marshal nodded and took another glance around the room before resuming. 'Sadie tells me you were askin' about Slim Freeman.'

'That's right.'

'Might I ask why?'

'Slim's an old friend. I happened to see him just the other day—'

'That's impossible,' the marshal interrupted. 'I'm sorry to have to say it, but I'm afraid Slim died. About four months ago. You could visit his grave. It's easy to find up on Boot Hill.'

'I've seen it already.'

'Well, there you are. It must have been somebody else you saw. It's an easy mistake to make, especially if you've not seen Freeman in a long time.'

'I never said that.'

The marshal gave him a quick, searching glance.

'As I recall, Slim was pretty ordinary lookin'. Nothing much to distinguish him.'

'Tell me,' Tyler replied. 'Just how did Slim die?'

'Natural causes. There was nothin' unusual or suspicious about it.'

There was a pause which the marshal used to get to his feet.

'Enjoy your stay,' he said. 'In addition to the Spur, I can recommend the Hatch Saloon in Hervey Street. The best Old Berry Bourbon west of Lost River. And if you're lookin' for good food, you could do worse than the Can-Can restaurant – give their oysters a try.'

32

Stepping into the passage-way, he stopped for a moment.

'Don't forget to hand over those guns.'

'Take 'em now if you want.'

'Later will be fine. I'll tell my deputy to expect you.'

With a nod he turned on his heel and walked quickly away to the head of the stairs. As he descended, he was soon lost from view. Tyler went back into the room, closing the door behind him. He walked over to the balcony and looked down. The marshal was making his way up the street, past the Spur saloon where a number of horses were drawn up at the hitch-rack. Were any of the trail hands still in town or had the drive travelled further on? He thought for a moment about going across but changed his mind. For some reason, he felt reluctant to face another encounter with Sadie Roundtree. The afternoon was well advanced. The hotel dining room would be open but he didn't feel like sticking around. For a moment he considered taking the marshal at his word and sampling the delights of the Can-Can restaurant but he wasn't particularly hungry. He felt a strange restlessness. He took a last look up and down the street. The marshal had disappeared. He turned back into the room and sat astride the chair for a while. He tried to think, but his thoughts were jumbled. Time passed. Finally, he got up from the chair, strapped his gun belt round his waist, and went out, locking the door behind him.

It didn't take long to reach the marshal's office. The marshal wasn't there, but as he had said, his deputy was. By contrast to the marshal, he seemed very young. His name was Brinkley and he seemed to have been well briefed; he knew what Tyler had come for before he had even said anything about it. Tyler handed over his guns and quickly left. Without his .44s, he felt oddly vulnerable, as if it wasn't something extraneous to himself he had left behind, but some vital part of him. A lot of towns operated a similar policy and it wasn't the first time he had had to check in his sidearms, but it made no difference.

He wandered about aimlessly for a little while till, retracing his steps, he passed by the marshal's office again. As he approached, a curtain was suddenly quickly drawn across the lighted window. He paused for a moment and then walked away again. Without having consciously made a decision, he eventually found his steps were leading him towards the cemetery. It lay on rising ground just on the edge of town; over the entrance hung the bleached skull of a Longhorn. He passed beneath it and slowly made his way among leaning headstones and tumbledown crosses. In a prominent place stood the tombstone purportedly belonging to Slim Freeman. He bent down to examine it more closely, and in the instant he did so he heard the report of a rifle and a bullet whined close by him, ricocheting from another nearby headstone and sending up shards and splinters of rock. He crouched down, taking shelter

34

behind the headstone as two more shots rang out, screeching and singing among the tombstones like wailing banshees. Rolling away, he got to his feet and began to run as hard as he could, doubled over to make himself less of a target and cursing because he had handed over his six-guns. Another shot rang out but he was beneath the crest of a rise with the river unwinding like a silken skein beneath him. Suddenly his foot slipped and he went rolling and tumbling down the slope. He struggled to his feet again, taking a moment to recover. Then he ran on till he was among the willow trees and aspens which lined the river bank. There were no more shots and he felt more secure but continued running pell-mell till he was confident that he must have left his assailant well behind. He slowed to a jog and then a walk before stopping altogether as he fought to find his breath.

Once he had done so and the danger was over, he felt a surge of emotion composed of a mixture of anger, shame, and self loathing. It wasn't like him to run, and it made little difference to tell himself that he had no choice. He should have known better than to hand over his weapons and render himself defenceless. After all, it wasn't as if he hadn't been warned. Somebody had been in his hotel room. How could he have been so stupid? He thought of the marshal. Was it just chance that he had been a target immediately after disarming himself? Maybe the marshal himself had fired those shots. But why? What was going on? What had he got caught up in?

He carried on walking, blind with rage and resentment, barely noticing that night had fallen. The stars came out and were reflected in the turgid waters of the river. A chill breeze began to sough among the trees. There was a splash nearby and then another as something slithered into the water. After a time he saw the dark outline of another island in the middle of the river and as he got nearer he could discern the dim, uncertain shape of something drawn up on a beach. He strained his eyes to see through the darkness and finally saw that it was the hulk of an abandoned riverboat. It lay on its side, partly obscured by vegetation with only its tall smokestacks outlined sharply against the sky. As he looked, he thought he detected a faint glow which seemed to emanate from its interior. He was intrigued and his anger began to subside. He stepped up his pace till he came alongside the head of the island when he stopped and climbed down the riverbank to the edge of the water. Rather than increase in intensity, the glow he had detected had subsided and he came to the conclusion that it was the last dying embers of a fire. Someone must be camping out on the island. He was about to leave it at that and had already started to climb back to the path and retrace his steps when he stopped. His curiosity was aroused. Who could it be? He looked about for evidence of a boat but could see nothing save the overhanging vegetation. The island was separated from the mainland by only a short stretch of water. Taking off his shoes, he stepped into the river and began to wade out, but had only gone a short way when the ground slipped away beneath his feet. He stumbled but quickly regained his equilibrium. A variety of sounds reached his ears, eerie suggestions of slithering and splashing. Could there be alligators? He began to have second thoughts about reaching the island when his ears picked out another sound, and this time it certainly wasn't made by any creature. It was the sound of footsteps, still some little way off but unmistakable. Someone was coming along the path he had just left and there was little doubt in his mind that he was being followed. Why else would anyone be there at that deserted spot in the middle of the night? He had assumed he had thrown off whoever had taken those shots at him, but apparently he was wrong. For just a moment he hesitated and then, tying his shoes together and putting them round his neck, he slipped into the water and began to swim, slowly and silently, towards the island.

The water was cold and he felt the weight of his clothes, but he was a good swimmer. He hadn't gone far when a ripple passed over the water and he looked about in dread of seeing an alligator. He had an empty feeling in the pit of his stomach but there was no choice other than to carry on swimming. He had been lying on his stomach but now he turned over on to his back and continued that way, keeping one eye on the riverbank. He moved smoothly through the water, taking care not to make any unnecessary noise. The stars shone down from a black sky and threw points of light on the placid waters. He was thankful that there was no moon which might have given enough light to betray him. He moved into a section of darker water and realized he was in the shadow of the wrecked riverboat. Presently it overhung him like the ribs and bones of a defunct sea monster. The effect was unsettling. He felt even more exposed and threatened. Then he caught a gleam of light along the shore which quickly vanished. He assumed it was a momentary reflection from something metallic, perhaps a belt buckle or even the barrel of a gun. He turned his head and saw that the current had carried him some little distance downstream. He was close to the island now and began to look for a suitable spot at which he might come to shore. The banks were high and trees over-hung the water. He relaxed his strokes and allowed himself to drift a little further till he saw what he was looking for; a break in the riverbank and a thin line of shingle. Turning over once more, he resumed swimming on his stomach, breaking the surface of the water with powerful strokes which brought him closer to the beach. Then his feet touched bottom and he rose up, splashing his way out of the river. The stones felt hard on his feet and it was with some discomfort that he finally reached the line of trees and sank down on the grass.

He lay for some time without moving, feeling the effect of his exertions. It seemed like a long, long time since the marshal had visited him in his hotel room. Things had certainly turned out differently from what he might have expected. He was finally aroused by the feeling of cold which began to creep over him. The night was still quite warm but he was wet and his clothes clung to him. He dragged himself to his feet and was about to move when the snap of a twig halted him in his tracks. His first thought was that it must be his pursuer, but a moment's reflection was enough to convince him that it couldn't be him. The idea was absurd; there was no way the man, whoever he was, could have crossed over to the island. Automatically, he reached for his guns till he remembered he no longer had them. Before he could do anything else a voice spoke, low and firm.

'Don't move. Whoever you are. I've got you covered.'

He turned in the direction of the voice and in another moment the bushes parted and a figure emerged with a six-gun in its hand. The man halted for a moment, and then came towards Tyler. The night was dark and Tyler could not make out his features, but as he got closer he thought he detected something vaguely familiar about him. It was more a general impression, something about the way he moved, but as he came near and he could begin to see his face more clearly, the sense of recognition grew stronger. Then he let out an involuntary gasp.

'Freeman!' he breathed. 'Hell, I don't believe it. Is it really you?'

Diamondback Casey's lean-to shelter at the back of the Spur Saloon wasn't a whole lot better than the shack to which he had taken Tyler, but he was grateful for Sadie Roundtree for letting him live in it. Before she had taken pity on him he had been really down and out, so that on more than one occasion he had looked back with gratitude to the times he had been in jail for vagrancy. At least then he had a roof over his head and meals. Now, though, he felt things were really looking up. He had a place to stay, he had a job and now he had an added purpose in life. He couldn't have said why, but he had taken to Tyler and he intended taking Tyler up on his suggestion that he keep his ear to the ground. He wasn't sure what was going on, but something was and he intended to find out more. In this he wasn't being entirely selfless. No; if he could manipulate things to his own advantage, so much the better. He stood to gain.

It was in that frame of mind that he took out the pack of Bull Durham Tyler had given him and proceeded to build himself a smoke. Sitting in the doorway, enjoying the afternoon sun as it streamed into the yard, he finished the cigarette and then rolled another. He had just about finished it and was beginning to nod off when a shadow fell over him and he snapped to attention. It was Sadie Roundtree.

'Don't mind my interrupting,' she said.

'Sorry, ma'am. Just takin' a break.'

'A long one. Seems to me you've been making yourself scarce today.'

He took a last drag on the cigarette in order to give himself space to think.

'I ain't due to be on duty till later, ma'am,' he said.

'I had a little job for you earlier. You weren't here.'

It didn't take much insight to persuade him that it wouldn't be a good idea to let his boss know he'd been riding out with Tyler. After all, he had told him what he knew about Freeman and shown her story to be false. Had she seen him in Tyler's company? He didn't think so.

'Sorry, ma'am. There were a few things. . . I needed. . . .'

'You bought yourself some tobacco?' she said.

'Yes. No. That is, I keep it here. I try to make it last.'

'Well, that's your business.' She seemed to relent and smiled faintly.

'Is there anything you want?' he asked. 'Is there anything I can do?'

'It's all right,' she replied. 'You've got a right to relax now and then, same as the rest of us. I'll see you later.'

'Sure thing, ma'am.'

She made as if to go but then turned back again.

'Just one thing,' she said. 'There's a new person in town. You might have noticed him in the saloon last night. He goes by the name of Tyler. I was just thinking. . . if you were to hear anything, pick up any information about him, I'd be grateful if you'd let me know.'

'Yes, of course. Any particular kind of information?'

'Oh, anything really. Nothing in particular, but I'm sure you'd agree it's only sensible to be wary when a new person arrives in town. I know it's nothing, but I noticed, for example, that he was carrying sidearms. I expect he'll be handing them in, but you can't be too careful.'

Diamondback nodded. He felt he had rode his luck already a little and was glad when she was gone. He waited a while and then got to his feet. He went to a makeshift cabinet nailed to one wall and got down a dusty bottle containing a few drops of whiskey and tipped it back. His nerves steadied themselves. He felt he had handled a potentially awkward situation quite well. It was strange, though, that Sadie and Tyler should both have asked him to find out information. He was more convinced than ever that something was afoot, something from which he might make even further gains than he had been reckoning on already. He would need to be careful though. If he mishandled things, he might lose the very benefits he had just been congratulating himself about.

CHAPTER THREE

Tyler was feeling a lot better than he had when Freeman first appeared. That wasn't difficult. At that point he had been at his lowest ebb; wet, exhausted and disorientated. In fact, he couldn't be certain that Freeman himself wasn't just an apparition, a figment of his weary brain. He didn't have to concern himself about the matter, however, because Freeman, taking a firm grasp of the situation, had wasted no time in getting Tyler back to his hideout in the wreck of the riverboat. Tyler had been right in identifying the glow he had seen as the last remnants of a campfire, and Freeman quickly built it up again while Tyler exchanged his soaking garments for some spare duds Freeman had supplied. Now, with a mug of coffee laced with whiskey inside him and a cigarette between his fingers, Tyler felt almost human again. His glance took in the rippling waters of the river in which he had been so recently immersed, the surrounding woods and, when he leaned back, the massive frame of the riverboat looming over them.

'Sure is an unlikely set-up,' he murmured.

Freeman laughed and looked up at the wreck himself.

'Tomorrow, when it's light, I'll show you around the place,' he said. 'There wouldn't be much point right now.'

'You mean you actually live in it?'

'It's kinda higgledy-piggledy, but it suits me. In fact, I can think of a lot worse places.'

Tyler took a pull on his cigarette before looking closely at his companion.

'Perhaps you'd better tell me what's goin' on,' he said.

'Not till you tell me just what in tarnation you're doin' here.'

Tyler nodded.

'OK. That's fair. There ain't much to say in any case.'

'You turn up here out of the blue after takin' a midnight swim in alligator infested waters, and you tell there ain't much to say.'

Tyler took another drag.

'It's like this,' he said. 'I was at a loose end. I kinda got to thinkin' about the old days and figured I might just as well ride out this way as any other. I had a vague idea I might run into you but it was nothin' much more than that. As it turned out, I did see you.'

'When was that?'

'A few days ago. I couldn't make contact at the time so I decided to stick around. A town like Green

Fork . . . I figured I'd be pretty sure to run into you again.'

'As simple as that?'

'As simple as that.'

'Nothin' more?'

Freeman thought for a moment.

'Maybe,' he said. 'In any event, what I didn't take into account was finding your grave stone up on Boot Hill.'

Freeman didn't interrupt and Tyler quickly outlined what had happened since then. When he had finished it was Freeman's turn to be thoughtful.

'Someone took a shot at you?' he queried.

'Yeah. And like I say, whoever it was, he followed me. That's why I took to the water.'

Freeman let out a muffled laugh.

'I'm not sure that was the best choice.'

'I didn't have much option,' Tyler said. 'I had no guns.'

'Well, you don't have to worry any further about that. I can fix you up with a couple of .44s.'

Freeman glanced at him.

'You've got artillery?' he said.

'Sure. I can let you have a rifle as well. I'm prepared.'

'Prepared for what?'

Freeman laughed again, this time more loudly.

'Definitely not for you puttin' in an appearance,' he replied.

'I might take up your offer,' Tyler said. 'But first of

all I'm going to pay that deputy marshal a visit and see about getting my own guns out of hock.'

There was a pause. Both men were beginning to feel relaxed, enjoying the stillness and peace of the night. Freeman took the coffee pot and refilled their mugs.

'Go on then,' Tyler said eventually. 'I've told you my story. Now tell me yours.'

Freeman took a swig of coffee and placed his mug on the ground.

'You asked me just now about bein' prepared for somethin'. I think you can probably guess what.'

'You tell me.'

'Maybe you'll recall that those varmints we put behind bars are due for release round about now?'

Freeman's hand stroked his stubbled chin. He looked at his companion.

'The Lassiter gang? I can't say I'd given it much thought,' he said. 'But I guess you're right.'

'I'm right. And I'll tell you why I'm right. Because just like you saw me, I saw one of them. At least, I'm pretty sure I did. And if there's one, there'll be others.'

'When was this? Recently?'

'A few months back. I couldn't be certain. That whole business with the Lassiters was a long time ago now. But when you've been shot by somebody, you tend to remember.'

'You figure it was just chance?'

'It could be, but I think not. Those boys swore to

get revenge. It seemed like too much of a coincidence. So, I figured I'd better get ready in case someone paid me a visit. Nothin' happened. Then I came home one evening and found my place on fire.

'I managed to put it out, but I figured I needed to do somethin'. I didn't like the idea of just waiting around, makin' myself a sitting duck.'

Tyler took another drag on his cigarette before flicking the stub into the fire.

'I think I'm beginnin' to get the picture,' he said.

'I faked my death. With a little help from my friends.'

'That don't seem like your way.'

'Don't get me wrong. I'm just buyin' myself a little space. I ain't foolin' myself those varmints won't figure things out, just like you have. Sooner or later they'll start askin' around, and when they do, I'll have flushed them out. I'll know who and how many I'm dealin' with. I'll be ready for the time of reckoning.'

'There's at least one person ready to spill the beans already,' Tyler said.

'Yeah? Who's that?'

'An old timer by name of Casey.'

This time Freeman laughed louder than ever.

'Old Diamondback!' he exclaimed. 'He's all right. What did you give him? A quart of Tarantula Juice?'

'Somethin' like that.' Tyler paused before going on. 'He took me to some tumbledown old shack. Figured he'd seen you there.'

47

Freeman looked quickly into Tyler's face and then turned away again.

'I ain't hidin' anything from you. There's no point. I was at that old cabin for a purpose.'

'Let me guess,' Tyler said. 'You were lookin' for somewhere to hide what's left of the loot.'

Freeman looked at him sharply.

'You know?'

'Sure. Leastways, I had a pretty good idea. The last time I saw you, you told me you were goin' to look for it.'

'Well, I found it. I would have contacted you. You know half of it is yours.'

'You should have handed it back.'

'Maybe so. But no-one had an out and out claim to it, and I figured I was owed. Both of us were owed. We brought those varmints to justice and I got shot in the process.'

'I figure I'd remember that. After all, it was me that dug out the bullet.'

'I never had a chance to thank you. You lit out before I was back in the saddle.'

Tyler shrugged.

'I don't care about the money.' He stopped for a moment. 'But why did you hide it in the cabin? I assume that's what you were doin' there. Why not bring it here?'

'I don't know. It was the first place that occurred to me. I once lived in that old cabin. Of course, it wasn't like it is now. I called it home then.'

'Home?'

'Near enough. Near as I'm likely to get.'

Tyler glanced at him. He thought he caught something in the other's expression but if so it quickly vanished and after a moment he continued.

'So just let me know if I've got this straight. This whole charade is because you reckon the Lassiter boys are back in circulation and comin' to get you?'

'They swore revenge. And what's more, they'll be lookin' to get their hands on that loot.'

'The loot you just stashed away somewhere in that cabin?'

'That's about the size of it.'

There was another pause before Tyler asked, 'How many of 'em do you think are on your trail?'

'I don't know. There were eight in the original gang. Some might have died, some might have quit the owl hoot trail.'

'Somehow I don't think that's very likely.'

'OK. So if they've reformed and they're all still around, it could be eight. Might be more, might be less.'

'More?'

'They could have attracted new members. There are plenty of disaffected cowpokes and horse thieves lookin' for a home. Not to mention worse.'

It was the second time Freeman had used the term 'home'. There was nothing in that, but for some reason it registered with Tyler. He quickly put it aside.

49

'Are you sure you couldn't be wrong about this?'

'Somebody tried to burn my house down. I wasn't imaginin' that.'

'Yeah, and somebody tried to shoot me,' Tyler mused.

'That's very odd,' Freeman said. 'Any idea who it might have been?'

'I was inclined to put it down to the marshal or his deputy, but now I ain't so sure.'

'It wouldn't be the marshal,' Freeman replied. 'He's got his faults, but he ain't a bad man.'

'He might have assumed I was one of the Lassiter gang out to get you.'

They finished the last of the coffee and settled back, enjoying the warmth as the embers of the fire began to fade. At one point a piece of a branch suddenly spurted and blazed before dying away again. Eventually Tyler spoke.

'I'm still trying to take this all in,' he said, 'but there's one thing you can count on.'

'Oh yeah,' Freeman responded. 'And what's that?'

'Assumin' you're right about this, you won't be facing up to those Lassiter varmints alone. You've got me alongside you now.'

Freeman turned to him.

'I sure appreciate that,' he said, after a moment. 'Hell, it'll be like old times.'

Tyler grinned.

'Let's hope for the same outcome,' he said. 'Apart from you gettin' plugged, that is. But right now I reckon I could use a little shuteye.'

'Me too,' Freeman said.

He tossed the last dregs of the coffee on to the embers, dousing them.

'See you in the mornin',' he muttered.

The sun had set behind the hills and the valley was filling with shadows as the herd was finally bedded down for the night. The first watch had been set and those cowboys not on duty were drinking coffee around the campfire. They had left the town of Green Fork behind them and they had a long way to go before the next one. The odour of the herd was strong, but the men scarcely noticed it. Somewhere a cow coughed and from time to time the slow monotonous chant of the cowboys singing to the herd drifted to their ears. After a couple of hours, the first riders on guard duty came riding back to camp to be relieved by the second watch. They took their places by the fire and someone produced a harmonica, put it to his lips and began to play. The sound was at once warm and lonesome above the hushed voices of the men. The song finished and the man embarked on another tune. Some of the men began to sing along as they slipped into a relaxed mood of reminiscence tinged with nostalgia. When the man had come to the end of his final tune, he shook his harmonica and replaced it inside his coat.

'Reckon I'll be turning in now, boys,' he drawled and walked away to spread his bedroll and make a pillow for his head with his saddle. Some of the others began to do likewise. As they settled down to sleep, from far away the complaint of a coyote rose upon the still night air. A horse snickered. The night was huge and quiet.

Suddenly the silence was shattered to smithereens by loud whoops and yells and the rattle of gunfire. Stabs of flame illumined the night. With one accord the cattle were on their feet, bawling and snorting in panic. Some of them were a fraction of a second too late, and down they went under the lunging bodies of their kind, shoving and stumbling over them. The entire herd began running with the wind, but soon the cattle began to circle in order to run against it. The men ran to retrieve their horses from the remuda and set off in pursuit.

Like a mighty rushing torrent, the maddened cattle thundered across the prairie, running down and trampling anything that lay in their path. Above the thunder of hoofs, the crack of gunshots rang out and spurts of flame continued to stab the darkness. The cattle plunged on but the men had gained on them and their horses were now running alongside the distraught beasts. Amidst the confusion the men kept firing their six-shooters, attempting to turn them. It seemed a useless enterprise, but the beeves were still fairly compact and running on a wide front rather than splitting into separate groups. If the men could hold them together, they might regain control as the cattle tired. They had to keep the animals running straight. There were more flashes from the men's .45s. It seemed to have a slight effect as the leaders started to turn, but the press of panicking beasts was too great and the herd kept on at the same breakneck speed.

The men were now stretched out in a line as they attempted to form a cordon, and indeed the herd was beginning to string out. If they could just swing the leaders into a wide curve they might be able to wind them closer and closer together. Suddenly they were entangled in a thicket of mesquite. Some of it was high but mostly it was shrub size. A little further and then they were out in the open again. The cattle, temporarily checked, resumed their running pace but were now scattered into a number of different bunches. The men fired their six-guns into the ground in front of them. The steers began to turn and head the other way, and as they did so the cowboys crowded them with their horses. The rear cattle continued to forge ahead and the result was that finally they started to circle. Once they had a mill going, the men knew they were back in control.

Watching the proceedings from a high point overlooking the valley, Mort Lassiter with four of his henchmen sat their mounts and laughed till they were hoarse. It was only when the stampeding herd was out of sight that they began to calm down.

'Hell, I ain't had so much fun in a long time,' one of the men remarked.

'How about we ride on down there and help ourselves to some supplies?' another one said.

'Leave it,' Mort remarked. 'There's a few of 'em still left. They might not have taken kindly to those beeves gettin' scattered.'

He looked back in the direction of the cattlemen's camp. In the dim light thrown by the lantern on the chuck-wagon, he could see dim shapes moving about.

'We'll get all the fun we want once we hit town,' another man commented.

Lassiter turned to him.

'You sure will,' he said. 'But remember what we've come for. First we deal with Freeman. Then we celebrate.'

A murmur of voices greeted his remark.

'Just wait till I get my hands on him.'

'That piece of buffalo dung has got it comin'.'

'Simmer down, boys,' Lassiter said. 'We've got to find him first.'

'Maybe Jed and Lucas will have traced him by now.'

'Ain't no point in speculatin',' Lassiter replied. 'We'll find out soon enough.'

They waited just a little while longer till Lassiter turned to two of the riders behind him.

'You did a good job stampedin' those cow critters,' he said. 'You put on quite a show.'

'It was a real pleasure, boss,' one of them replied. There was a further brief guffaw of laughter.

'Well, if your horses are rested, I don't see much point in hangin' about here any longer. I'd say it was time we moved on.'

Without more ado, Lassiter dug his spurs into his horse's flanks. With a last glance at the scene below, the others followed suit and they rode away, headed for Green Fork.

Tyler woke late to the smell of bacon sizzling in the skillet and the aroma of coffee.

'Right on time,' Freeman said.

He forked the bacon on the plates and poured the coffee.

'It's a beautiful morning,' he said.

'If you don't mind me sayin' so, for a man in hidin' you don't seem to be takin' too many precautions.'

'There's a reason for that.'

Tyler threw him a quizzical look.

'Like you mentioned last night, hidin' out ain't really my style. Since I decided to fake my death, I've been havin' second thoughts. Seems to me it might be a better idea to let the Lassiter boys find me. Now I'm about ready for 'em.'

'Have you already taken some measures?'

'Not as such. Maybe we could work on that. I figured this old riverboat is defence enough. I'll show you around once we've finished here.'

The island proved to be bigger than Tyler had envisaged. It was well wooded and separated by a decent width of water apart from one point at the far end where a rocky spur ran close to the opposite shore from which Freeman had approached it. The main feature, however, was the wrecked boat itself. It had settled in such a way that, with a little effort, Freeman and Tyler were able to scramble about inside it. In what had been the main saloon, Freeman had established himself almost in comfort. He had rescued some items of furniture and set himself up where a collection of broken and smashed furnishings surmounted by what had been a bar formed a relatively level surface. Everything else was pitched at an angle and at first Tyler felt disorientated and slightly giddy.

'You soon get used to it,' Freeman said.

'What happened to the boat?' Tyler asked.

Freeman shrugged.

'Just ran aground I guess. The place must have been ransacked long ago. I was lucky anythin' was left.'

They came outside and climbed along the hull where the name of the riverboat was inscribed in huge red letters: *Elenore*.

'Wonder who she was?' Freeman remarked.

At the stern the broken paddle wheel rose into the air at a crazy angle.

'I don't know much about these things,' Freeman commented, 'but it looks to me like she's engineered so the floats enter and leave the water at right angles.'

'What's the purpose of that?'

'Makes it go faster.'

'Didn't do her much good,' Tyler said. 'She'd have done better to go slower.'

'She ain't goin' anywhere now, fast or slow, that's for sure,' Freeman said. 'Leastways her boiler didn't blow up. That's often the way they go.'

They hauled themselves over the rail of the upper deck. The two smokestacks stretched their long necks below them, lying partly athwart and partly concealed by the rapidly enveloping vegetation.

'I reckon we could hold out here for a long time, no matter what numbers Lassiter might throw at us.'

'What have you got in the way of artillery?'

'Plenty. And supplies enough for a siege.'

Tyler's gaze swept over the island. The sun was getting stronger and swarms of flies were hovering in the air. The sluggish river looked green; it carried tree branches and other detritus from upstream and formed little whirlpools over the shallows and sand-bars.

'Talkin' of guns,' he said, 'reminds me; I mean to pay a visit to the deputy marshal.'

'Today?'

'Tomorrow will do.'

'Be careful what you're doin'.'

'I thought you said Marshal Dick was OK?'

'The marshal is, but I ain't so sure about his deputy. But that wasn't my meanin'.'

'What was your meanin'?'

'Do you need to ask? Somebody already took a few shots at you, and we're both agreed that the Lassiter gang are on their way. I'm pretty sure I've already seen one of the varmints. It's just a question of time till the rest of 'em get here.'

'While I'm in town, I'll see if I can find out anything.'

'You got somewhere to stay?'

'I'm booked in at the Franconia Hotel.'

Freeman thought for a moment.

'Try Diamondback,' he said. 'He's got his nose to the ground.'

'Where would I find him?'

'He lives in a lean-to at the back of the Spur Saloon.'

Tyler considered Freeman's words.

'I'm surprised,' he said. 'I wouldn't have thought Sadie Roundtree would be happy with a situation like that.'

'Sadie Roundtree can be a surprisin' person,' Freeman replied.

Tyler didn't respond because he had been struck by a sudden thought.

'Just one thing,' he said after a moment.

'Yeah?'

'How do I get back across the river?'

Freeman laughed.

'Don't worry,' he said. 'You won't have to swim. How do you think I get across? There's a ford. In any case, the water ain't nearly as deep as it looks.'

They took a last long look at their strange surroundings and then began to clamber down.

Although Freeman had worked out the best way to do it, it wasn't easy and Tyler was relieved when they reached the ground. They worked their way to the far end of the island where the river was narrower.

'This is it,' Freeman said. 'A horse could wade across without too much difficulty.'

'There's just one thing you seem to have forgot. I haven't got a horse.'

'You don't need a horse.'

Tyler regarded the river closely.

'I sure don't want to end up as some alligator's lunch,' he said.

Freeman laughed.

'Don't worry,' he said. 'Take a look at those bushes by the water's edge. There's a canoe.'

They walked to where it was partly concealed and drew it out.

'It doesn't look any too watertight,' Tyler remarked.

'I've used it a few times. In any case, you haven't got far to go.'

They dragged the canoe the few yards to the water. Tyler got in and Freeman handed him the paddle.

'Sure you don't fancy a trip to town?' Tyler said.

'Nope. Not just at the moment anyway. You figure on comin' back anytime soon?'

'Depends on what happens in town,' Tyler replied.

'Make sure you conceal the canoe,' Freeman said. 'I don't want any other visitors for the moment.'

'How is your impression of a hoot owl?' Freeman asked.

Tyler looked at him with a puzzled expression.

'We need some sort of signal. So I'll know it's you and not someone else.'

Tyler nodded and gave a half-hearted bird impression.

'It wouldn't fool an Indian,' Freeman said, 'but it'll do.'

With a grin, Tyler pushed himself away from the shore. The boat quickly got caught in the current and he had been swept along a little way before he managed to swing it round and into midstream. When he looked back at the cove, Freeman had already disappeared. Suddenly he felt light-hearted. The sun glanced on the water and broke into dazzling reflections. He felt a sense of freedom which was magnified by the strangeness of his situation. There was something unreal about it. He felt ready for whatever else might be coming his way.

CHAPTER FOUR

Marshal Dick was looking at some Wanted posters when the door flung open and his deputy burst into the room.

'What is it?' he snapped.

'Better step outside,' Brinkley replied.

He got up from his chair and walked quickly to the door. He looked one way, towards the Spur Saloon, but could see nothing untoward. When he looked the other way, however, he saw a troop of riders approaching. They were riding abreast so that they dominated the street and anyone crossing had taken refuge on the sidewalks. They watched in trepidation as the riders passed, their horses' hoofs kicking up clouds of dust.

'Looks to me like they spell trouble,' Brinkley said.

Without replying, the marshal stepped off the boardwalk and took up a position in the middle of the street. The riders bore down on him and were almost upon him before they drew rein. The leader looked down.

'What's the problem, Marshal?' he said.

'No problem.'

'Then maybe you should step aside. It ain't real healthy standin' in the road like that.'

'I'm the one handin' out the health warnin',' Dick replied. 'This is a quiet town. I aim to keep it that way. So if you were thinkin' of causin' a disturbance, then don't.'

Lassiter swivelled round to face his men.

'You hear that?' he called. 'The marshal don't want any disturbance.'

His words were greeted by guffaws of laughter as he turned back.

'I don't know what you mean,' he said to the marshal. 'Do we look like the kind of people that would cause a disturbance?' There were further gusts of merriment before he went on:

'We're just passin' through, Marshal. Nice to have met you though.'

The marshal's eyes were steely as they swept the ranks of the riders.

'As long as we understand one another,' he said.

With a further glance, he stepped back up to the boardwalk and after a few moments the men rode on again. He turned, expecting to find Brinkley, but to his surprise the deputy marshal wasn't there. When he entered the office, he found him standing by the window.

'I had you covered,' he said.

The marshal gave him a quizzical glance.

'That's good to know,' he replied.

Brinkley hesitated a moment before moving away from the window and asking, 'You figure they spell trouble?'

The marshal shrugged. 'As long as you're there to cover me, I guess I can deal with it.'

'What about their guns?'

'I didn't want to take a chance right there on the street with so many people around. Maybe what he said was true.'

'What was that?'

'That they're just passing through. If it's not, we'll just have to keep a close eye on 'em. We'll see how it goes. If nothin' happens and they're still around tomorrow, we can decide if anythin' else needs to be done.'

Brinkley paused.

'Who do you think they are?' he asked after a moment.

'I don't know.'

'You think they might have somethin' to do with Freeman?'

'Freeman wasn't exactly forthcoming about his reasons for wanting to drop out of sight,' the marshal replied, 'but it's a fair bet he wanted to avoid somebody. Maybe this is just a coincidence. Maybe there's nothin' in it. On the other hand. . . .'

He glanced through the doorway. The dust kicked up by the riders' horses still hung in the air.

'You don't mind if I leave you in charge for a while?' the marshal asked.

'Of course not. I'm about due to take over anyhow.'

'I think I'll just take a little walk over to the Spur Saloon,' Dick said. 'In case those boys decide to return later, I'd better warn Miss Roundtree.'

He turned and walked away. While he and Brinkley had been talking, the street had come back to life. Pedestrians who had taken shelter from the horsemen had emerged from their places of concealment and while Dick surveyed the scene, a buckboard and then a wagon appeared at opposite ends of the street. A lone horseman came round a corner, dismounted, and tied his horse to a hitchrack outside the grocery store. A dog cocked his leg and urinated against a stanchion. With a grin, the marshal set off for the Spur Saloon.

When Dick was gone, Brinkley sat down at his desk. The Wanted posters were still where Dick had left them and he browsed through them in a desultory way. Suddenly he came to attention. He recognized the portrait. It was Jute Lassiter. Involuntarily, he looked up, a guilty expression on his face, as if he expected to see the marshal there. Then he carefully folded the poster and put it into his pocket. He got up and began to walk round the room, but he was feeling unsettled. He had just sat down again when the door opened and a man stepped inside. He was facing into the sunlight streaming through the windows and for a moment Brinkley couldn't see who it was. Then he recognized Tyler. He gave a start. Without ceremony, Tyler took the cane-backed chair opposite Brinkley and sat astride it.

'You seem a mite surprised to see me,' he said.

'I'm not surprised. I just didn't expect you back so quickly.'

'Maybe you didn't expect me back at all.'

'What is that supposed to mean?'

'Shortly after I left you yesterday evening, someone took a shot at me. I don't suppose you'd know anything about it?'

Tyler was looking closely at the deputy marshal to see if he could detect any giveaway signs, but the young lawman, after his initial indication of surprise, seemed to have regained his composure.

'I'm sorry, but I don't quite get what you're drivin' at,' he said.

Tyler relented.

'It's OK,' he said. 'I wasn't drivin' at anything. But the fact remains that somebody tried to dry-gulch me and I mean to find out who it was.'

'I'm sorry about that, but I can assure you I had nothing to do with it.'

Tyler threw him a questioning glance.

'I'll take your word for it,' he said.

'I'll keep my ear to the ground,' Brinkley replied. 'If I hear anything, I'll be sure to let you know.'

Tyler nodded and then turned to look up at the

wall. His gun belt and .44s were still hanging there.

'I've come to get my guns back,' he said.

'I've already told you, it's illegal to carry a weapon.'

'I don't care about any ordinance the marshal might have laid down. I want my guns back. I was caught out yesterday. I don't intend lettin' it happen again.'

Tyler and the deputy marshal exchanged glances. Brinkley looked away and shifted in his chair before getting to his feet and walking over to the peg on the wall. He reached for Tyler's gun belt and then handed it across the desk.

'I wouldn't usually do this,' he said, 'but I guess you've got a point. But don't think you can get away with anythin'.'

'Much obliged. I won't,' Tyler replied.

He rose to his feet and fastened the gun belt round his waist. The deputy marshal watched him before suddenly turning the conversation in another direction.

'You got here just a bit too late,' he said.

'What do you mean? Too late for what?' Tyler asked.

'To be honest, it was no great shakes.'

'What wasn't?'

'A bunch of horsemen came ridin' through. Not long ago.'

'A bunch of horsemen? So what?'

'You tell me. Don't get me wrong. They didn't do

66

anythin' amiss. But they were kinda menacing, if you know what I mean.'

'Did you recognize any of them?'

Brinkley shook his head.

'Nope. I don't figure they were from any place around here.'

'How many?'

'Half a dozen or more. That in itself is a little unusual.'

'They could have been trail hands. I gather you get bunches of them comin' into town.'

'The latest herd already passed by. Besides, they didn't look like trail hands.'

Tyler stroked his chin. He was wondering why Brinkley seemed to be getting some kind of a kick out of referring to the matter.

'Oh well,' he concluded. 'If they pose any kind of threat, I guess that's your problem. Yours and the marshal's.'

Again, Brinkley and Tyler exchanged glances. Each of them had a feeling that there was more to the other's comments than was obvious, but neither could work out what it might be. Tyler made for the door.

'Thanks for lettin' me have my guns back,' he said. 'And don't worry. I ain't some kind of gunslinger. I won't be the cause of any trouble.'

For a moment he filled the doorframe and then he was gone. Brinkley went over to the window and glanced out. For some reason, he expected Tyler to be heading for the Spur Saloon, but in fact he was walking in the opposite direction.

Tyler fully intended paying a visit to Diamondback, but first of all he wanted to get his horse from the stables. There might be problems getting it across the river, but he figured he might be needing it. In his experience the town ostler was usually a good source of information, and he had a question or two in mind for him as well. At the same time, Brinkley's comments had set him thinking. He and Freeman were half expecting a visit at some point from the Lassiter gang. Could they already be here? The answer to that was pretty obviously in the positive. Quite apart from the riders Brinkley had just told him about, there remained the fact that he had been shot at. He was pretty certain none of the Lassiter boys had been involved in the search of his room. He suspected that either the marshal or Miss Roundtree was behind that; maybe both of them. Or could it have been Brinkley? There was something about the deputy marshal that didn't sit right. He had been surprised at the ease with which Brinkley had given him back his guns. He certainly seemed to sit loose to the letter of the law. Why was that? If it was the marshal or Miss Roundtree who had carried out the search, their motives might well have been good ones, in the sense that they were looking out for Freeman. Maybe they had assumed he might be a member of the Lassiter gang. When he had spoken with Sadie

Roundtree or the barman, they had certainly given precious little away.

When he reached the livery stables, it was to find the ostler forking hay. He looked up at Tyler's approach.

'Howdy,' he said. 'I figured you'd be here before now.'

Tyler leaned against a rail.

'Why do you say that?'

'Simply because your sidekick saddled up and rode out some time ago.'

'You mean Casey?'

'Old Diamondback. Yes, of course that's who I mean.'

Tyler pondered his words for a moment.

'Did he say where he was goin'?'

'As a matter of fact, he did. He told me he was taking a ride up into the hills.'

'Did he say where in the hills?'

'Nope. That was it.'

Tyler had been intending to visit the Spur Saloon to have a word with Diamondback. Now there didn't seem to be much point. He glanced over his shoulder where his horse stood in its stall.

'Is my sorrel ready?' he asked.

'Sure. She's fed and groomed. All you got to do is saddle her up.'

Tyler made to move then stopped.

'You haven't had any customers recently?' he asked.

'No more than the usual.'

'You ain't had anybody today?'

'Nope. Things are quiet at the moment.'

Tyler nodded. It didn't take him long to saddle up and as he led his horse out of the livery stables, the ostler was still forking hay.

Marshal Dick's entry to the Spur Saloon was greeted by a slight diminution in the level of noise but it was only momentary and the place had quickly resumed its raucous atmosphere as he glided swiftly up the stairs. He reached the landing and as he approached Sadie's door it opened and the lady herself appeared.

'I was looking out the window. I saw you comin'.'

He slipped inside.

'You've been here for a while?' he asked.

She nodded.

'Then maybe you saw that gang of horsemen come ridin' through?'

'Yes, I did. Is that why you're here?'

Without waiting for an answer she moved to a cabinet and took from it a bottle and two glasses.

'Brandy,' she said. 'And not just any old brand.'

'Thanks. I sure could use a glass.'

She poured and as she did so he came behind her and put his arms round her waist.

'Sorry,' he said. 'I almost forgot. Things must be really getting to me.'

She smiled and they kissed.

'Come and sit beside me,' she said, 'and tell me

what's on your mind.'

They sat together on a chaise longue. After he had taken a sip of the brandy he turned to her.

'I didn't like the look of those riders,' he said.

'Me, neither,' she replied. 'From what I could see of them out of my window.'

'A bunch of men ridin' together like that, it ain't usual.'

She looked at him closely.

'Are you thinkin' there could be a connection with Freeman?'

'I'd say it was a pretty safe bet. Wouldn't you?'

'We might be jumpin' to conclusions. Freeman was very reluctant to give much away. More than that, he made it pretty clear that whatever it was he was mixed up in, he didn't want anyone else to get involved.'

She took a sip of the brandy.

'More to the point,' she said. 'Do you even know where Freeman is?'

The marshal shook his head.

'He's liable to turn up sometime. Or I could get up some sort of search party. I guess it wouldn't take too long to find him.'

'I don't think he'd appreciate that,' Sadie said. 'We've known Freeman long enough to know he can take care of himself. I think we need to trust that he knew what he was doing when he decided to lie low. Making a fuss trying to find him wouldn't be very sensible.'

The marshal finished his glass and Sadie poured another.

'I don't know,' he said. 'I just don't know. I've got a bad feelin' about this whole thing. Especially since I need to be out of town for a few days.'

'Out of town?'

'Yeah. Remember – I told you about that funeral in Normansville. Old Lucas.'

'Oh yes. You wouldn't want to miss that.'

'I didn't know him too well, but us old lawmen got to present a united front.'

'I wouldn't worry too much. Nothing is likely to develop in that time and besides, Brinkley is capable of looking after the show while you're gone.'

'It ain't that I'm worried about.'

He put his glass down and approached her.

'I'm sure you'll be able to cope,' she said. 'Still, I don't like to see you like this. Maybe I can help make you feel better.'

He smiled and, getting to her feet, she came close and began to undo the top button of his shirt.

'You could certainly try,' he replied.

It wasn't hard for Tyler to pick up the trail left by the Lassiter gang. There wasn't much doubt in his mind that was who the riders were. It wasn't long since they had hit town so he couldn't be far behind them. Their sign was easy to follow. In addition, he thought he had a pretty good idea about which way they would be heading. His previous experience with them was enough to lead him to believe they would seek a hideout in the hills, a sort of hole-in-the-wall from which they could direct their nefarious operations. That was the way they had operated previously and he had no reason to believe they would do otherwise now. As he rode, he also kept half an eye open for Diamondback. The ostler had stated that the oldster had set off riding in that direction. Was it a coincidence or had Diamondback already picked up some information which caused him to set off that way? It was certainly a stroke of luck that the Lassiters had opted, out of bravado he supposed, to ride through town. If Freeman was taking few precautions, neither it seemed, were they.

When he had set off for Green Fork, he had anticipated that it might take him some time to locate them. Instead, they had played right into his hands and almost advised him of their whereabouts. He needed to be careful, though. He had been lucky once to survive being shot at. He might not be so lucky a second time, and it was certain that the Lassiter gang were not far ahead. At one point he thought that a faint smudge in the distance might be thrown up by their horses, but quickly discounted the idea when it disappeared. As he rode he kept checking the ground for their sign, but it was easy to see and he didn't need to stop and dismount in order to examine it at closer quarters. The line of the hills had appeared and he was congratulating himself on the good progress he had made when his eyes picked out the same slight discolouration on the horizon he had noticed previously, but this time in a different direction. At almost the same time, his ears picked up the sound of hoof-beats. He brought his horse to a stop and listened carefully. He regretted that he didn't have his usual field-glasses in his saddle-bags but his keen vision soon detected the distant shapes of riders. There were three of them and he quickly decided that they were a splinter-group of the main party he had been following. What did it signify? Could they have somehow realized they were being followed? It didn't seem very likely. Nevertheless, if he was right, the riders had detached themselves from the rest of the gang and were coming at an angle in his general direction. He looked around. The country was rolling with patches of brush and clumps of trees. They offered plenty of opportunity for concealment. Spurring his horse, he rode a little way into shelter.

For a while nothing happened. He couldn't see any further indications of the horsemen and although he strained his ears for sounds, he could hear nothing. He had just about decided that there was nothing in it and that the riders he had seen must have simply been going about their business, when he again picked up the faint clatter of hoof-beats. They grew steadily louder, but as they got closer he was sure that this time they were made by a single rider. He moved slightly further forward so that he had a better view through the tangle of leaves, and presently there came into a view a lone horseman, riding hard. He was still some distance away, but after a few minutes Tyler thought he recognized him. It was Diamondback! Without thinking, he spurred his horse and emerged from cover.

Diamondback had ridden into a hollow but he quickly emerged. He was at an angle and had obviously not seen Tyler, who set off in pursuit. He realized immediately that he should have let the oldster get nearer, but it made little difference because he soon began to catch up. When he reflected that Diamondback was probably riding the horse that the ostler had picked out for him previously, it wasn't surprising. He was closing fast, but Diamondback still seemed oblivious of his presence. Tyler shouted as loud as he could, but the wind blew his words back into his face. Then, unexpectedly, Diamondback's horse suddenly stumbled and fell, throwing the oldster over its head. The horse was quickly back on its feet, but Diamondback lay immobile. Tyler covered the rest of the ground and leaped from the sorrel. He kneeled over Diamondback, fearing the worst, but the oldster was conscious and looked up at him with an expression that took Tyler aback till he realized it was because his glass eye had been jolted from its socket.

'Don't shoot me,' the oldster pleaded. His voice was shaky and he was obviously winded, but he didn't appear to have incurred any serious damage.

'Nobody's gonna shoot you, you old goat,' Tyler responded.

Diamondback stared up at him, his face contorted with a mixture of pain, shock and incomprehension, which slowly turned into one of confused surprise.

'I can't see too well,' he stuttered, 'but jumpin' Jehosaphat, is that you, Tyler?'

He began to struggle in an effort to sit up. Tyler put his arm around his shoulders and he put his own arms around Tyler's neck. Tyler tried to avoid looking too closely at his empty eye socket. When he had gained an upright position, the oldster seemed to realize for the first time that his glass eye was missing. Tyler glanced around. A glint from something on the ground attracted his attention and he detached himself from the oldster in order to check what it was. Sure enough, it proved to be Diamondback's glass eye. He handed it back to the oldster who proceeded to screw it back into his eye socket; again, Tyler preferred not to look too closely.

'Hell, that makes all the difference,' the oldster exclaimed when the process was completed.

'How can that be?' Tyler enquired.

'I don't know, but it does,' Diamondback replied.

He seemed a bit groggy and began looking around him vaguely. Suddenly he became animated and seized hold of Tyler's arm.

'Quick,' he said. 'There's no time to waste. They can't be far behind me.'

'Who can't be far behind you?'

'The riders,' he said. 'I tried to shake them off, but I don't think I did.'

As if to back up his words, Tyler became aware of the faint sound of hoofbeats. He wasn't too sure just what was happening, but it seemed the time for explanations would have to wait.

'Here,' he said to Diamondback, 'let me help you up.'

Once the oldster was back on his feet, Tyler retrieved his horse.

'Think you can ride?' he asked.

The oldster nodded and Tyler quickly helped him into the saddle. When he turned away, he knew it was too late. The sound of hoofs had steadily increased and now he caught his first glimpse of the horsemen. There were still three of them and they were coming on fast. Tyler glanced towards the trees but they were too far off for them to reach. Already they heard the first crack of a rifle.

'Get down again,' Tyler snapped.

He leaped from his own horse and half dragged, half lifted the oldster out of the saddle. Then, without hesitation, he deftly brought each horse to its knees and down on the ground. He and Diamondback took shelter behind their prone bodies, and Tyler drew his six-guns. The oldster followed his lead, and to Tyler's surprise, pulled a Sharps rifle from its scabbard. He watched as the oldster put it to his one good eye, took a moment to sight it, and then pulled the trigger. The report rang

out, booming above the patter of shots that were now
being rained on them by the fast approaching horsemen. The leader of the group flung up his hands and
went tumbling backwards out of the saddle. The
other two slowed, taken by surprise, giving Tyler the
opportunity to open fire with his six-guns. One horse
reared, unseating its rider, and when he saw that he
was the only one left, the third rider turned and
began to gallop away. The two riderless horses continued running, galloping past the spot where Tyler
and Diamondback were sheltering behind their own
mounts. The man who had taken the fall lay inert for
a few moments, and then suddenly got back to his
feet and began running towards the trees.
Diamondback raised his rifle but Tyler shouted at
him.

'Let him go. He's got a long walk ahead of him
before he reaches anywhere!'

They watched as the man continued running in a
blind panic till he was most of the way towards the
trees when Tyler finally arose and brought the fright-
ened horses to their feet again, whispering to them
and stroking them in order to calm them down.
When he looked towards the trees, the fugitive had
disappeared. Carefully, he approached the man
Diamondback had shot but it was immediately clear
that he was dead. Tyler turned to the oldster.

'That was some shooting,' said. 'You got him
plumb between the eyes.'

The oldster spat.

'You know, he said, 'it's a funny thing but I figure I only really started shootin' straight when I was down to one eye.'

Tyler looked away and his eyes swept the horizon.

'You've got some explainin' to do,' he said, turning his attention back to Diamondback.

'Sure I have. But I figure we ought to get away from here. For all I know, there could be more of the varmints followin' on behind these three.'

'Are you sure you're up to ridin'?' Tyler asked.

'Yeah. I'm fine.'

They mounted their horses but Tyler quickly got down again.

'What are you doin?' Diamondback said.

Tyler bent down and looked closely at the dead man's boot.

'Just a thought,' he replied.

The sole of the man's boot didn't match the impression left by the intruder to his hotel room. All the same, he was pretty sure now that some member of the Lassiter gang was responsible. He must have been in the Spur Saloon that night and, like Diamondback, overheard something of his conversation with Sadie Roundtree, or picked up his information from the bartender. He hadn't wasted any time. It was almost certainly the same man who had taken those shots at him. It didn't seem too likely, but he would certainly like to catch up with him some day.

'What do we do about him?' Diamondback asked.

'You just said there could be others followin' on behind. Let them deal with him.'

Tyler swung back into the saddle as Diamondback looked at him ascant.

'You ain't said what you're doin' out this way,' the oldster remarked.

'That can wait too. Right now, let's head back to town.'

Tyler felt rather reluctant to give up the trail he had set out to follow. But he was concerned about the oldster and at the same time he didn't feel like pushing their luck. From what he could gather, if they delayed they might find themselves up against even bigger odds. Besides, he could always return to the trail. In the meantime, he was eager to hear what Diamondback might have to tell him. Without further comment, he touched his spurs to the sorrel's flanks and began to ride away, with Diamondback close behind him.

They rode steadily, paying close attention to any indications of further trouble. They were following the route Tyler had just covered, heading for town, but as they got closer Tyler began to have second thoughts and to wonder whether it might not be better to make for Freeman's island hideout instead. It had advantages. He had a feeling it might be sensible not to be seen around town and for the time being he wanted to avoid any contact with Sadie. On the other hand, it would mean blowing Freeman's cover, but then Freeman himself didn't appear to be too concerned about remaining out of sight. If he and Diamondback were to exchange confidences, it would be hard to avoid telling him. In the end he decided for the town option, at least for the moment.

All the same, when they finally got there, he felt decidedly uncomfortable and instead of following Diamondback's lead and making for the livery stable and then the Spur Saloon, they left their horses tied outside the Franconia Hotel and made their way to the dining room. As they passed the reception desk, the clerk drew Tyler's attention.

'I'm glad I caught you,' he said. He reached down to a shelf below the level of the desk and produced an envelope.

'A note for you,' he said. 'Mr Brinkley, the deputy marshal, dropped it in earlier.'

Tyler took the envelope and glanced briefly at it before placing it in his pocket.

'Thanks,' he acknowledged.

The afternoon was well spent but it was still relatively early and there was only a thin scattering of residents taking their meal. Satisfied that they would be safe from the prying eyes of anyone they knew, Tyler led the way to a corner table and they both sat down. Diamondback glanced about him with a shifty expression; he was clearly unused to such luxuries.

'I sure could do justice to a decent steak,' Tyler said. 'How about you?'

'Yeah. Sure. All that ridin' and shootin' has got me kinda hungry.'

81

'Don't talk too loud,' Tyler advised. For some reason he felt jumpy. Again the thought passed across his mind that it might have been better to head for Freeman's island after all.

The waiter approached and Tyler ordered for them both. While they waited for their food, he outlined in as few words as possible what had happened since he last saw the oldster. When he got to the part about Freeman's hideout, the oldster grinned and let out a hoarse chuckle.

'I should have figured it,' he said.

'Make sure you keep it to yourself,' Tyler said. 'Maybe I shouldn't even have said anything.'

'You can trust me,' Diamondback replied. 'Why would I want to nose it abroad anyway?'

Tyler had no answer to that. He continued his account and when he had finished he looked closely at his companion.

'OK,' he said. 'Now it's your turn.'

The oldster scratched his chin but before he could begin the waiter appeared with two juicy steaks with the trimmings. Diamondback's mouth positively drooled. To Tyler's surprise, he carefully tucked a napkin around his scrawny neck before tucking in. Tyler didn't interrupt his enjoyment. He was too occupied in his own steak. Only when they were halfway through did he bring the oldster's attention back to the matter in hand.

'There's not much to say really,' Diamondback said. 'Like you asked me, I kept my ear to the ground and it didn't take me too long to find out that a stranger in town had been asking questions about Freeman. Someone said he rode a chestnut mare with a blaze. I paid a visit to the livery stables but it wasn't there. It was just luck that I saw it tied outside the general store one day next to a buckboard. I waited around till the stranger appeared. He was with another man and a woman—'

'The woman,' Tyler interrupted. 'Was she young or old? Did you recognize any of them?'

'I guess she must have been about thirty. I don't know; I was concentratin' on what was happenin'.'

'What was happenin'?'

'They were carrying a number of parcels. They loaded them on the buckboard and then the man and the woman climbed aboard and they drove off.'

'What about the other man, the one with the horse?'

'He went back inside the shop. After a minute or two he reappeared and began to walk down the street. I followed him. He went to the barber shop. I figured I had time to collect my horse. By the time I'd done that he came out, walked back to the grocery store, got aboard his horse and rode off.'

'You were careful not to be seen?'

'Sure. I might be old but I ain't stupid. In any case, he went off in the same direction as the buckboard. Between them, they made a trail a greenhorn could have followed.'

He paused as if for effect.

'But here's the really interestin' bit,' he said. 'After a time the rider caught up with the buckboard and then they all carried on right up into those hills. I was wonderin' where on earth they could be headed, but I pretty soon found out. There are some old cabins up there. I guess they must have been used by miners or diggers. They're pretty much rundown – a bit like the one I took you to – but they're bein' used again. That buckboard stopped right outside one of 'em.'

'How do you know that?'

'Like I said, I ain't stupid. I left my horse tethered in a safe spot and crept up on 'em on foot. There's plenty of cover. I watched while they unloaded the buckboard. Afterwards they all went inside. I hung around for a bit but I started to get jittery and decided it was time to pull out. It was when I was clear of the hills and well on my way back that those riders must have spotted me.'

'You figure they were the same ones you followed?'

'One of 'em certainly was. The one I shot. He was the stranger on the chestnut mare.'

'Something must have happened to make them suspicious. Either they heard you or came across your sign. It was lucky I came by when I did.'

Tyler paused, gathering his thoughts.

'It all adds up,' he concluded. 'That gang of riders whose trail I was following must have been heading for the outlaw roost in the hills that you spotted. That can only mean that they are all in one gang – the Lassiter gang, and they're closing in on Freeman.'

He paused to reflect for a moment.

'I'm pretty sure now that it was somebody connected with the gang who took those shots at me. At first I thought it might be someone whose loyalty was to Freeman and who took me to be a member of the gang. That could still be the case, but I don't think so.'

'Either way, you could still be in danger.'

Tyler regarded the oldster, turning matters over in his mind. Could the shot conceivably have come from him? Was that the reason he had been hiding in the bushes that first night when he had given himself away by stumbling over the cask? Despite his glass eye, he had proved himself a good shot in the encounter with his pursuers, and those bullets had gone mighty close. On the other hand, why would he have been so willing to help him find Freeman? He put the thought from him, fairly sure that he could trust the oldster. After all, Freeman had given him his recommendation. It was much more likely that it was one of the Lassiter gang. All the same, it might be an idea to keep tabs on him and not give him any further opportunity. That was why he came to the conclusion that, rather than remain in town, they should both make for Freeman's island. However, the prospect of crossing over in the dark was not one he relished. It would be better to leave it till the next day. In the meantime, he would stay overnight at the hotel and leave the oldster to make his own way to his cabin at the back of the Spur Saloon. Even if the oldster was up to something, there was not much he could do overnight. When he suggested they ride together to the island early the next morning, the oldster became quite animated.

'By Jiminy,' he said, 'I was hopin' you'd say that.'

'Is that so?'

'Sure. I've been hanging around this town doin' nothin' for so long, I'd just about forgotten there was any other way.'

They exchanged glances and Tyler grinned.

'Finish that steak,' he said, 'and I'll order us some coffee.'

CHAPTER FIVE

Marshal Dick had just emerged from his office and was about to get on his horse for the ride to Normansville when three horsemen came riding up. They dismounted and tied their horses to the hitch-rail before approaching him.

'Don't I recognize you boys from somewhere?' he asked.

One of them took the lead.

'We're with the Bar 8,' he said.'

Dick nodded. 'Yeah. You passed through just a day or two back.'

'That's right. My name's Bonner, by the way. I'm trail boss.'

'Glad to make your acquaintance. But shouldn't you be headed for the Flat River?'

'Yup. The fact is, though, there's been some delay.'

'Delay?'

The trail boss exchanged glances with his companions before replying.

'A bunch of no-good desperados scattered the herd.'

'That's right,' one of the men added. 'They rode right in by night and set off a stampede.'

A light began to dawn behind the marshal's eyes.

'I see. I wonder if they could have been the same bunch came ridin' hell for leather through here, scarin' folks plumb silly,' he said.

The trail boss smiled.

'Then you'll understand that we don't take this kinda thing too lightly.' He seemed to relax and held out his hand.

'I'm glad we've met like this 'cause it saves me havin' to make a special effort. The plain fact of the matter is, we've got no intention of allowin' these coyotes to get away with it. We don't want to break no laws, but that's the way things stand. And to show our good-will, we're lettin' you know the situation.'

'This town is my jurisdiction,' Dick replied. 'Maybe it'd be better if you leave things to me. So far, I'm not sure that any ordinances have been broken.'

'I don't know nothin' about any ordinances. We don't mean to cause any trouble, exceptin' what's comin' to those varmints.'

The marshal nodded.

'I won't ask you to check in your guns,' he said. 'Just don't go shootin' 'em around Green Fork.'

The trail boss nodded.

'I don't suppose you know somewhere we might put up for a night or two?'

Dick thought rapidly. He had no reason to be suspicious of Bonner. In fact, he liked the cut of him. He could put some custom Sadie's way. He had no objections to them staying in town, at least so long as it was brief. At the same time, a little gentle encouragement might persuade them not to overstay their welcome. His main concern as marshal was to minimize the risk of any trouble while he was absent. Better to avoid it altogether than to have to clear it up once it got started.

'You could try the Magnolia on East Street,' he said. 'It's about the best guest house in town.'

'Thanks. I think we might do that,' Bonner replied.

He turned away and he and his men remounted.

The marshal watched them till they turned a corner and then got astride his own horse. He sat there for a moment, wondering whether to have a word with Sadie at the saloon, before finally touching his spurs to the horse's flanks and riding away himself, but not without some misgivings.

When Tyler and Diamondback, on their way to Freeman's island, reached the spot at which the canoe had been hidden, they faced a quandary. If they rowed over to the island, they would have to leave their horses behind. On the other hand, they were reluctant to trust the horses to wade across. In the end they chose the latter. Freeman had been right about the ford; although both horses were carried a little way downstream they kept their feet and made it to the other side without mishap. As they emerged from the water Freeman himself appeared.

'You found the crossing then,' he called.

They came up on to the shore and dismounted.

'I guess you could call it that,' Tyler replied.

Freeman glanced at Diamondback.

'I didn't expect to see you, old-timer,' he said.

'Hope you don't mind me bringin' him along,' Tyler said. 'We'll tell you the story just as soon as we see to these horses.'

'Bring 'em along,' Freeman said. 'I've got bacon in the skillet and coffee on the boil. I figure you could use some.'

They made their way to the wrecked riverboat. As they got close, Diamondback was clearly impressed.

'I remember her goin' aground,' he said. 'Musta been fifteen years ago or more. It were a stormy night. Most of the folk survived though.'

'I'll take that as a good omen,' Freeman replied.

He had a fire blazing and after the horses were dried and fed, they sat beside it and drank coffee while the bacon sizzled in the pan.

'This is right homely,' the oldster commented.

'I guess it depends what sort of home you got in mind,' Freeman said.

The bacon was ready and he shovelled it on battered old tin plates. While they ate, Tyler quickly described what had happened since he left the island. When he had finished Freeman was quite animated.

'Things are falling into place,' he said. 'Looks like we were right about the Lassiter boys. The only question now is, do we wait for them to show up here, or do we go after them?'

'Ain't you jumpin' the gun a bit?' Tyler said.

'What do you mean?'

'Well, we still can't be certain about Lassiter.'

'What other explanation is there? What else do we need to know?'

'Nobody's broke any laws yet. What about the marshal? He might have something to say about all this.'

'You were shot at, weren't you? That's proof enough for me.'

'He's got a point there,' Diamondback remarked to Tyler.

'They came after Diamondback. Hell, he shot one of 'em. Looks to me like war has already been declared.'

Tyler shifted uncomfortably, but he had to admit that Freeman was right. They were slap bang in the middle of something and there was no other way but to see it through.

He thought for a moment before replying. 'OK, but I figure we should let the Lassiters make the first move. That way there'll be no question about who's in the right and who's in the wrong.'

'You mean we should wait here and see how things develop?'

'That's right. And while we're waiting, we can be

digging ourselves in so we're ready for them if and when they do show up.'

'We've got supplies and ammunition,' Freeman said.

'They'd be hard pushed to take us by surprise,' Diamondback commented. 'This place is like a stronghold.'

Freeman turned to him.

'You don't have to stay,' he said. 'This is my quarrel.'

'Mine too,' Tyler interjected.

Freeman smiled.

'Yes, yours too. But you don't need to get involved and maybe get yourself killed.'

'Ain't you forgettin' already what you just said? I shot one of 'em. I'd say I was as involved as the two of you now.'

Freeman pondered his words for a moment.

'I guess so,' he admitted. 'Well, looks like we're all together in this. So, that's three of us. How many of them?'

'At least a dozen, I'd say, judging by what the deputy marshal was sayin' and what we've found out for ourselves. There could be more of the varmints on their way.'

'We'd better assume the worst.'

'We might be well outnumbered, but Diamondback is right about this place bein' a fortress,' Tyler said. 'Somehow, I don't think any of the Lassiter boys are goin' to relish crossin' that ford.'

They broke into laughter.

'We could do with some rain up in those hills,' Freeman mused. 'The fuller the river, the better.'

Diamondback looked up at the riverboat looming over them.

'At least we got an ark,' he said.

He turned to Tyler.

'By the way,' he said, 'what was in that note the deputy marshal left?'

'Hell,' Tyler replied, 'I clean forgot about it!'

He put his hand in his pocket and drew out the envelope.

'I'm not sure I trust that deputy,' Freeman remarked. 'I was surprised Dick ever gave him a job.'

'I've known him since he was kid,' Diamondback said. 'He was always a bit sly. When the other kids got into trouble, he always seemed to avoid it, although I figure he was behind some of their worst pranks.'

'Maybe that's the reason the marshal took him on,' Tyler said. 'Give the kid a break.'

'You could be right,' Freeman added. 'He's a good man. It would be the sort of thing he might do.'

Tyler opened the envelope and unfolded a piece of paper from inside.

'Go on then,' Diamondback said. 'Tell us what it says.'

'Here, take a look yourself. He just writes that he's got some information that might be of interest and to drop by and see him next time I'm in town.'

'Information?' Freeman said. 'Information about what?'

'I don't know. Last time I saw Brinkley, he said he'd let me know if he heard anything about who took those shots at me. Maybe that's what it's all about.'

'Pity you forgot about the letter. You could have stopped by before we left town,' Diamondback said.

'Yeah, I guess so. Still, it's not far.'

'You're goin' back?'

'If not today, then tomorrow. If there's anything we need, I could pick it up while I'm there. I could have done without havin' to cross that ford again though.'

Freeman laughed.

'That ford is fine,' he said. 'Just ask your horse.'

At the Magnolia Guest House the three men from the Bar 8 were sitting on the porch enjoying a smoke.

'That sure was some meal,' Bonner remarked.

'Best chow since we hit the trail.'

'Makes me almost glad those varmints caused the stampede. I figure that latest cook we took on could use a few lessons.'

They sat in silence for a while till the sound of footsteps on the wooden floor announced the arrival of Sadie Roundtree.

'Coffee,' she announced.

She carried a tray with a steaming coffee pot and four mugs which she set down on a small table.

'Don't mind if I join you, gents?' she said.

They straightened themselves up.

'Of course not. We were just complimenting you on that meal.'

'Don't thank me,' she said. 'I had nothing to do with it. I employ a girl from the town to do the cooking.'

She sat down on a vacant seat and poured the coffee.

'This is nice,' she said. 'Of course I've seen some of you boys from . . . what was it again?'

'The Bar 8, ma'am.'

'That's right. The Bar 8. But this is different. Of course, you're welcome at the Spur Saloon any time. Maybe this evening if you feel that way inclined.'

'Thank you, ma'am. We might just take a stroll in that direction.'

'The Bar 8? I don't think I've heard the name. Are you boys up from the Gulf country?'

'San Antonio way.'

'Well, I guess it's a lot of hard travelling.' She paused for a moment before continuing. 'If you don't mind me asking; if you're in the middle of trail driving, then what are you doing here?'

Bonner exchanged glances with his companions before telling her briefly what had happened.

'A stampede?' she said. 'And you don't think it was accidental?'

'That's correct,' Bonner replied. 'It was no accident. A bunch of riders came in at night makin' a lot of noise.'

95

'Maybe they didn't realize you were there.'

'They knew it all right. They were just out to cause trouble.'

'Have you any idea who they were?'

Bonner didn't reply immediately and one of the others broke in.

'We sure aim to find out.'

Bonner took up his coffee mug but set it down again without drinking.

'I imagine you know these parts pretty well,' he said.

'I think you could safely say that.'

'Then have you any idea who might have done it?'

He regarded Sadie closely, looking for a reaction, but there wasn't any because she was in control of the conversation, having deliberately steered it in the direction she wanted.

'I think I may have. A bunch of riders came through recently,' she said, echoing the marshal's words. 'They caused some disturbance. It wouldn't surprise me if they were the same ones that set off the stampede.'

'Did you recognize any of 'em?'

'No. I'm pretty sure they were not from round here.'

'Are they still in town?'

'I wouldn't think so. If you ask me, they were just passing through.'

Bonner considered her words for a few seconds.

'Is there any place they'd be likely to be headed?'

'The next town is Cranesborough.'

'That's quite a way, isn't it? I think we saw it signed off further back down the trail.'

'It's a little way, but it's bigger than Green Fork.'

Bonner took a sip of his coffee.

'Well,' he concluded, 'I reckon we'll just have to wait and see. Maybe they'll be back here. Maybe – I don't know. I'll need to think about it.'

'Think about what exactly?'

'How to meet up with 'em of course. Sorry, I kinda took that for granted.'

'Don't you need to get back on the trail?' Sadie replied.

'We do. But I figure we can take some time out. After all, we don't want the same thing to happen again. That's a possibility too as long as these varmints ain't dealt with.'

'You'd be taking quite a risk. If I'm right about those riders, there are a lot more of them than there are of you.'

'Don't worry, ma'am,' one of the other men broke in. 'We know how to handle ourselves.'

'Well, I hope you do,' Sadie said.

Silence descended. A slice of moon showed in the afternoon sky above an angle of the rooftop and from somewhere among the trees a bird called. Eventually Sadie pushed aside her chair.

'If you gentlemen are finished with the coffee,' she said, 'I'll take these things back indoors.'

She placed the mugs carefully on the tray and,

with a smile, made her departure. The men from the
Bar 8 watched her as she closed the door and went
inside.

'I figure that's quite a lady,' one of them
remarked.

The other two remained silent till Bonner spoke
again.

'I don't reckon we're likely to run into any of those
varmints that run off the herd,' he said, 'but I guess
there's a possibility. What do you say we put in an
appearance at the Spur Saloon?'

'You figure that's where they would be? If they're
still in town, I mean.'

'Where else would they be?'

'The lady said she thought they were just passin''
through.'

'Maybe so, but there's no harm in checking out
the saloon. I'm sure none of us are averse to a drink?
Kind of round off the day.'

'How would we know them anyway?'

'A good question,' Bonner replied. 'I can't rightly
say, but somehow I think we just might.'

Although the cabin which Mort Lassiter had chosen
as his headquarters was the pick of the bunch, it was
nevertheless very basic and run-down. After years
spent in the penitentiary, however, it seemed almost
luxurious. In any event he didn't intend spending
much time in the vicinity of Green Fork – just long
enough to wreak his revenge on Slim Freeman and

to collect what was left of the loot the Lassiter boys had gathered in their previous incarnation. He had no doubts about succeeding in his mission. He might even have time for a bit of additional fun; maybe holding up the bank in Green Fork or just painting the town red. As he sat outside with a glass of whiskey in one hand and a cheroot in the other, he was exercising his mind in working out just what was the best way to go about things. It seemed fairly clear that in order to find the money, he would first need to get his hands on Freeman. Once he had extracted the information he needed, he could dispose of that individual – but not until he had made him suffer first. In fact, the two things could be very nicely combined. But where was Freeman? It seemed to him that the problem was not too difficult. It should be possible to ascertain his whereabouts with the use of a little force, a little cunning.

His cabin lay at the head of the trail leading up into the hills. From where he sat he had a good view of it winding its way down towards the plain. Presently his attention was drawn to the appearance of a horse which seemed to be carrying two riders. They were still a good way off, but as they got closer he thought he recognized them. They were two of his own men. They came slowly up the slope till they reached level ground when they stopped, dropped wearily from the saddle and approached him.

'What the hell is this, Harrison?' Lassiter rapped,

stubbing out the remains of his cheroot under his boot.

The man so addressed was still holding the horse's reins when another man appeared from round the corner of Lassiter's hut and without ado took them from him and led the horse away.

'You'd better have a good story to account for this,' Lassiter said.

'We got dry-gulched,' Harrison lied. He looked at the other man.

'Ainsworth's horse got shot. We didn't stand a chance.' He paused.

'Get on with it,' Lassiter snapped.

'It happened like this. We spotted someone snooping around so we gave chase. We didn't realize it was a trap. We'd nearly caught up with him when a bunch of riders came out of hiding and opened fire on us. Lawton was with us as well. They killed him.'

'Lawton?' Lassiter racked his brain but couldn't think of who Lawton was.

'We fought back but there was just too many of 'em.'

Lassiter stared at them long and hard.

'I'm not sure your story adds up,' he said.

Both men blanched but Harrison thought he saw his chance to clinch matters in his own favour.

'There's something else you ought to know,' he said. 'I can't be sure, but I thought I recognized one of them. It was a long time ago. I might be wrong.'

'I'm losin' patience.'

'I'm pretty sure it was Ry Tyler.'

Lassiter's face broke into a devilish grin.

'I can see right through you, Harrison. You think you're gonna get round me by bringin' me some information.'

'I swear it's true. About Tyler. About everythin'.'

Lassiter licked his lips. He was enjoying this. Suddenly his hand dropped to his belt and a six-gun appeared.

'Don't go shootin' us,' Harrison pleaded. 'I'm tellin' you the plain truth. We put up a show but we were outnumbered.'

Lassiter extended his arm and pointed the gun at Harrison's chest.

'Please,' Harrison stuttered. The other man opened his mouth to say something but the words wouldn't come. For just a moment Lassiter enjoyed the men's discomfort before he lowered his aim and put the gun back in his belt.

'You ain't bringin' me any news. You ain't tellin' me anything I didn't know already.'

Both men looked blank.

'I know perfectly well that Tyler is around. We had that information from Brinkley.'

'Brinkley?'

'Ah, I was forgettin'. You probably don't know Brinkley. He's the deputy marshal of that fly-blown town. Green Fork I mean.'

The expression on the men's faces was blank. They were still in a state of shock from Lassiter threatening them with his six-gun and were completely in the dark about what he was now telling them.

'Man, you're more slow-witted than a drunken mule. You didn't think I'd bring you all this far without havin' made some preparations? My brother Jute has been in town for weeks now, checking things out. Brinkley is in his pay. He's our man. He told Jute about Tyler and he's pretty sure he knows where Freeman is hiding. Tyler would have been a dead man before now if only Jute could shoot straight. If what you're tellin' me is true, then that's all the more reason for taking care of Tyler.'

He chuckled grimly.

'What's more,' he continued, unable to halt his flow of words, 'I've already got a little plan in place to get my hands on Tyler. It's just as well Jute missed him. The way I'm plannin' it now, Tyler is going to suffer. A bullet is too good for that polecat.'

His face broke into an ugly grimace.

'I'll make them both suffer,' he said. 'They've had it comin' to them.'

He stopped and was quiet for a moment, as if relishing thoughts of the treatment he would mete out to them. Then his expression relaxed and he looked at the two men in front of him as if he only just noticed them.

'Go on,' he said. 'Get out of my sight. But if you've been lying. . . .' The sentence lay unfinished and the victims of his wrath didn't waste any time in waiting to hear it completed. Quickly they made their exit and after a moment Lassiter resumed his former relaxed posture and took up his unfinished drink. Only a faint smile which played about the corner of his mouth betrayed his evil thoughts.

He was still turning things over in his mind when the door of the cabin opened and a woman came out. He looked up at her approach.

'What are you doing?' she asked.

'Oh, just thinkin'.'

'About us?'

'Yes, of course. What else would I be thinkin' about?'

She gave a little laugh and sat on his lap.

'I don't believe a word of it,' she said.

He grinned.

'Then I'll tell you what I was thinkin' about. I'm thinkin' about just how good things are gonna be once we've settled with Freeman and got our hands on that loot.'

'Promise you're gonna take me back East to all those fancy stores.'

'I've already done that.'

'Tell me again.'

He looked down on her and put one hand on her breast.

'Sure. We'll go to New York. We'll go to Boston. We'll buy ourselves houses and jewels and carriages. We'll move in society. Hell, we'll be the biggest swells in town.'

His other hand lifted her skirt and began to work its way up the inside of her leg.

'Just what do you think you're doing?' she quipped.

By way of reply he lowered his head to hers and kissed her open mouth. Their tongues met and when they finally drew apart she wriggled free of his hands.

'Come on,' she whispered. 'One of the men might come by. Let's go inside.'

He got to his feet and together, holding hands, they made their way inside the shack.

Tyler experienced no problems fording the river and arrived in town not long after leaving the island. He stopped outside the marshal's office, dismounted and tied his horse to the hitch-rack. Stepping up to the sidewalk, he knocked on the door.

'Come in!' a voice called.

He opened the door and was relieved to find Brinkley sitting at his desk. If it had been the marshal, he would have had to look further afield and his time might have been wasted. When he saw who his visitor was, Brinkley seemed slightly disconcerted.

'Tyler,' he said. 'What are you doin' here?'

'Haven't you forgotten something?' Tyler replied.

The deputy marshal suddenly seemed to come to his senses.

'Ah,' he said, 'I take it you got my note?'

'That's right. You seem a little surprised.'

'I've got a few things on my mind. I just forgot for a moment.'

He got to his feet and Tyler thought he was about to shake hands when, with a sudden movement, Brinkley drew his six-gun.

'Drop your gun belt,' Brinkley said.

'Haven't we already been through all this? I thought you said it was OK for me to have my guns back.'

'Let's just say something has come up to cause me to change my mind.'

'Does Marshal Dick know about this?'

'Never mind that. Just do as I say.'

Tyler thought for a moment of making a move but the deputy marshal's gun was pointed straight at his stomach. He reached down, unbuckled his belt and threw it to the floor. Brinkley stretched out a foot and kicked it aside. He nodded towards a door at the back of the room.

'Start walkin',' he said.

Tyler turned and shuffled slowly towards the doorway.

'Are you takin' me to the cells?' he said.

'Just keep goin'.'

'If I'm bein' arrested, perhaps you could tell me on what charge?'

'I don't have to tell you anything,' Brinkley replied.

They reached the door and Brinkley reached across to open it. Again, Tyler thought about making a move, but decided against it. Apart from more obvious considerations, he didn't want to get on the wrong side of the law, though he couldn't imagine what he had done wrong. For the present, it seemed that it might make sense to comply.

The door led to a dimly lit short corridor beyond which were the cells. There were only two of them, both unoccupied. Brinkley produced some keys and unlocked one.

'Get in!' he snapped.

'Aren't you goin' to tell me what this is all about?'

By way of reply, Brinkley gave Tyler a push in the back which propelled him though the open door which was instantly locked.

'Don't I have rights?' Tyler said.

'Shut up.'

'That note was a ploy, wasn't it? You don't want to see me about any information. You just wanted the opportunity to put me behind bars. Where's Marshal Dick?'

'The marshal is out of town at the moment. Not that it's any business of yours.'

'What's your game, Brinkley?'

'I told you to shut up.'

Brinkley moved away but couldn't resist a last comment.

'You'll find out soon enough,' he said.

The door to the outer office closed behind him and the cell was plunged even further into gloom and Tyler waited till his eyes adjusted. The only item of furniture was a bare metal bedframe and the main source of light was a barred window. By standing on the bedframe Tyler could just reach the bars with his outstretched arms. With an effort he succeeded in hauling himself high enough to be able to catch a brief glimpse of the outside world before falling back again. He tried once more with the same result. He didn't know what he was trying to achieve, it was more of an instinctive reaction. There was no chance of escape that way. The bars were solid and in any case the window space was too narrow. He sat down on the edge of the bedframe to consider the situation.

One thing was pretty clear. Unless he had transgressed some obscure ordinance, the deputy marshal was acting illegally and pursuing some private agenda of his own. He thought back to the previous conversation he had had about Brinkley. He had more or less disregarded what Freeman and Diamondback had said, but on consideration, they backed up what he recognized as his own feelings about the deputy marshal. He didn't trust him. What was Brinkley up to? Again, he thought about those shots that had been fired at him in the cemetery. Was that Brinkley after all? He still had his doubts about that. He had been with Brinkley not long before, when he had handed in his guns. Brinkley could have done something then; put him in jail or whatever. He recalled the curtain closing as he walked by. Hadn't he glimpsed a second person? Could the deputy marshal have been passing on information, setting up the ambush? The more he thought about it, the more likely it seemed. Brinkley had set him up and it was only by luck of the gunman's incompetence that he had survived. Assuming the bushwhacker was one of Lassiter's henchmen, then the deduction to be drawn was that Brinkley was on Lassiter's payroll. At first he felt excited at having worked things out, but his initial feeling was quickly replaced by another. If he was right, this stay in the cells could only be temporary. The only way Brinkley could be safe was to get rid of him. Maybe he was informing Lassiter of the situation right now. He looked up again at the barred window. If there was nothing to be gained there, he needed to think of another plan quickly. Almost certainly, his life depended on it.

CHAPTER SIX

After locking Tyler up, Brinkley returned to the front office. At first he was feeling quite pleased with himself. The plan had worked out well. All that remained was for Jute Lassiter to play his part, collect the prisoner and take him to wherever his brother and the rest of the gang were hiding out. When he sat down, however, he found his hands were shaking and as the minutes passed, he began to feel more and more nervous. Despite his better judgement, he felt uneasy with Tyler so close. He was there, just beyond the door that led to the cells. He felt his physical presence as though he was sitting next to him. It didn't matter that Tyler was helpless. He was still a disturbing actuality. And what if Marshal Dick decided to cut short or even abandon his trip to Normansville? How would he explain the situation? He glanced anxiously at the door. Evening shades were beginning to fill the room. It had all seemed so easy at the start when he only had Jute to deal with and the rest of the Lassiter gang were just a name. That was before Tyler had shown up to complicate matters. Maybe he had made a bad mistake getting involved.

Getting to his feet, with some difficulty because his hands were still unsteady, he lit a lamp. Then he resumed his seat, pulled open a drawer and drew out a half-empty bottle of whiskey. Without bothering about a glass, he took a swig from the bottle. A bead of sweat ran down the side of his face and there was a thudding in his ears. He glanced up. It was only the sound of the clock ticking. He took another swig and then a third, gulping as he placed the bottle on the table. Then he stood up and made for the door. For whatever reason, it was intolerable to remain. He had to do something, and after a moment's hesitation he decided that meant finding Jute Lassiter. He bent his steps towards the Spur Saloon, hoping he might find him there. When he came through the batwing doors, a sweeping glance around the smoke-filled room told him that Lassiter wasn't there. There were other saloons. Turning on his heels, he went back out and began to make his way towards Hervey Street and the Hash Saloon. It wasn't the sort of place Jute would be likely to frequent, but it was a possibility. Just being out and about was preferable to sitting alone in the marshal's office.

Although only brief, the deputy marshal's visit to the Silver Spur did not go unobserved. Sadie Roundtree had seen him enter and her quick instincts told her that something was not right. He had a haunted look about him. After a few moments' reflection, she crossed the room and stepped outside the batwings. She looked in both directions but Brinkley had gone. One thing she noticed, however, and that was the glow of lamplight in the marshal's office. It was still relatively early and it struck her as somewhat odd both that the lamp had been lit and that Brinkley had gone out without dousing it. She waited for a moment for a cart to pass by and then, picking up her skirts, she crossed the street. When she got to the marshal's office, she was further surprised to find that the door wasn't locked. She pushed it open and cautiously peered inside before entering. There was no sign of Brinkley but the empty bottle of whiskey still stood on the table. Although he was clearly not there, and she knew that the marshal was away, she gave way to a natural instinct and called out, 'Hello! Is there anyone here?'

To her surprise and consternation, there was an answering call.

'Hello!'

It came from the cells and was immediately followed by, 'I need help! Get me out of here!'

She halted, not sure how to react. She hadn't expected anyone to be occupying a cell. Who was it? Plucking up her courage, she took the lamp and holding it aloft, moved to the adjoining door. It was locked. She rattled the handle.

'Look for the keys!' the voice called.

She gathered her wits.

'Who is it?' she called. 'Why should I do anything to help you?'

'My name is Tyler.' There was a pause before the voice followed up with, 'Who is that?'

'Tyler!' she repeated, ignoring the question. She was confused. Tyler claimed to be Freeman's friend. What was he doing in the lock-up? Marshal Dick had certainly not mentioned anything about Tyler being under arrest. Presumably it was Brinkley who had arrested him. Could it be that Tyler was a member of the Lassiter gang? How would Brinkley know that? As she struggled to make sense of things, the outer door was suddenly flung open and Brinkley himself appeared. He stopped in his tracks, staring at the woman.

'Sadie!' he hissed. 'What are you doing here?'

There was a look about him that scared her but he gave her no chance to reply. Instead he strode quickly towards her. Even from that distance she could smell the whiskey on his breath. He came at her and made a motion as if to seize hold of her. Instinctively, she raised the lamp and brought it crashing down on his head. He stumbled backwards and made a motion as though to draw his gun. Without thinking, she stepped forward and hit him again. This time he stood swaying for a moment before crashing to the floor, banging his head hard against the corner of the desk in the process. She dropped the lamp and stood for a moment with her hand across her mouth, looking down at the inert form of the deputy marshal.

'Sadie!' a voice called. 'Are you all right? What's happened?'

She spun round.

'Brinkley,' she called. 'I think he's dead.'

'Who's dead?'

'Brinkley. The deputy marshal.'

There was a slight pause before the reply.

'Listen. Don't panic. This is what you must do.'

She hesitated.

'I can explain everything. Right now you have to get me out of here. I've got to get out of here. You've got to trust me.'

She was shaken, but in the next moment she knew what she must to do.

'Hold on!' she called. 'I'll have to find the keys.'

'They're probably on Brinkley's person.'

The light had gone out and it was hard to see. Reluctantly, she knelt down and ran her fingers across Brinkley's frame. She was in luck. The keys were in an inside pocket of his jacket. She drew them out and with trembling hands began to try one and then another in the locked door. At the third attempt the door opened and she stepped into the darkened corridor.

'It's all right,' Tyler said. 'Can you see me?'

She could just make out his shadowy form as it stood holding on to the bars. In a few seconds she was beside him and once she could see him more clearly, she no longer felt afraid. She selected a key and it fitted the lock. She turned it and the locked door opened and Tyler stepped free.

'Tell me I'm doing the right thing,' she said.

'You're doing the right thing and I'll explain why as we go along, but right now we need to get moving.'

'I think I've killed Brinkley.'

'What happened?'

'Come and see for yourself.'

He took her arm and together they made their way to the front office. A trickle of blood flowed from Brinkley's head, staining the carpet. Tyler kneeled down but quickly ascertained that the deputy marshal was not badly injured.

'He'll be OK,' he said.

Sadie seemed to visibly relax.

'Thank goodness for that,' she sighed. She reflected for a moment. 'Should we rouse the doc?'

'No time for that. He might have a bad headache when he comes round, but he'll survive.'

He got to his feet and looked round the room. His gun belt was hanging from a peg on the wall and he quickly retrieved it and strapped it round his waist.

'Pretty soon all hell is going to break loose around here,' he said, 'and unless we're careful, you're going to be one of its first victims.'

'How do you mean?'

Briefly, Tyler outlined what had happened to him. 'Brinkley is on the Lassiters' side,' he concluded.

'That letter he gave me was just a ploy to get me into his hands. Any time now some of the Lassiter boys are going to be turning up here to deal with me.'

'Do you know where Freeman is?'

'Yes, and that's where we had better be heading.'

'We?'

Tyler glanced down at the unconscious body on the floor.

'By what you've done to Brinkley, you've taken sides now. For your own safety's sake, you'd better come with me.'

Without further ado, he took her arm and they moved to the door. Tyler poked his head outside and quickly withdrew it.

'There's a bunch of men coming now,' he said.

'What should we do?'

'You know the marshal. Is there a back entrance to this place?'

'Yes.'

'Then let's use it.'

They swiftly crossed the room and went through the narrow corridor past the cells. Another passage led them to a back entrance.

'Try the keys,' Tyler snapped.

She held the keys up to her face.

'I know which one it is,' she said. 'It's this one.'

She inserted the key in the lock and opened the door. It was hard to see anything much. Tyler looked up and down but it was Sadie's turn to take the initiative. She quickly relocked the door.

'With any luck they won't even realize we came this way,' she said. 'This is an alley. One way leads back to the main street. The other way leads to a back street with a few offices and warehouses.'

She took his arm.

'Come on. I'll lead the way.'

Just for a moment Tyler held back.

'What is it?' she said.

'My horse. It's still tied to the hitch-rail out front.'

'Come back for it later.'

'We need to get away from town.'

She thought for a moment.

'I've got it,' she said. 'My boarding house is this way. I can pick up a few things while you collect your horse. I'll see you back at the Franconia.'

'Will I find it all right?'

'Just bear right at the end of the alley. You can't miss it.'

Their conversation was halted by sounds from the front of the building.

'Come on,' she said. 'Let's run.'

Without further hesitation they made their escape. At the end of the alley she turned to him.

'Be careful,' she said.

'Don't worry,' he replied. 'I'll just wait around till they clear off.'

She held his arm for a moment before walking quickly away. He watched her departing figure for a moment before ducking back down the alley. He had no intention of waiting around. He wanted to have a clearer idea of what was going on. Before he reached the end of the alley he could hear voices shouting and cursing. He flattened himself against the wall and peered out. Light was now streaming from the marshal's office and although he could not make out the words distinctly, it was clear that the people inside were arguing. After a few moments a figure burst from the doorway and began running down the street. His guess was that one of the Lassiter boys was going for the doctor. The voices were now more subdued but occasionally one rose above the rest. A few people appeared, moving towards the marshal's office. One of them stepped up and shouted though the doorway, 'Hello! What's happened? Can I help?'

Tyler was anxious for his safety but there was nothing he could do to prevent the man from stepping inside. If he was in any danger, he was saved by the arrival of other people on the scene. Quite a knot of people was gathering on the boardwalk and Tyler thought he saw his chance. He stepped out of the alley and approached them.

'What's goin' on?' he asked the nearest.

'Seems like the deputy marshal's been attacked and injured.'

'Really! That's bad. When did this happen? Who found him?'

'Some people happened to be passing by.'

'Are they in there now?'

'As far as I know.'

He turned away. All the people were interested in

what was happening inside the building. Nobody was concerned with him. Now was his chance. As non-chalantly as possible, he walked to the hitch rack and untied his horse. In a few seconds he was astride it but before he could get any further, the door to the marshal's office flew open and a couple of men appeared. Brushing aside the crowd, they advanced rapidly towards him. The leading figure had almost reached him when he looked up at Tyler. Their eyes met and, although the light was fading and he hadn't seen him for a number of years, Tyler recognized the ugly features of Jute Lassiter. Without further ado he touched his spurs to the horse's flanks and began to ride away. He didn't want to do anything which might draw further attention to himself, so he rode slowly, not deigning to look back. He didn't need to though, because almost immediately a voice rang out behind him, rapidly followed by the report of a gun. It made a loud noise, echoing around the buildings, and was followed by a second and a third shot. He felt the crump of the air but he was already riding hard. For the moment he was not concerned about which direction he was following. His one intent was to get clear of the guns booming in his rear. He saw a junction and turned down it. The sound of the shots faded in the lee of the buildings and he knew that for the moment he was safe. He didn't expect the Lassiters to try and pursue him. They had other matters to deal with. Even if they did, it would take time for them to find their horses and saddle up. No, the moment of danger had passed. He didn't need to change his plan. The safest option was to find the Franconia guest house as he had already arranged with Sadie. He turned another corner and continued riding more slowly, looking for the boarding house. He had no problem finding it. He rode a little further and then, not far ahead, he saw a group of people and horses gathered outside a house. When he got closer, he recognized Sadie Roundtree together with three men.

'Am I glad to see you,' she said. 'I heard shots. . . .'

'I'm fine,' he said, 'but we can't stick around for too long.' He glanced at the others.

'What's goin' on?' Tyler asked as he dismounted.

She smiled broadly.

'Let me introduce you. They all belong to an outfit called the Bar 8. Gentlemen, meet my friend Ry Tyler.'

He shook hands with the three of them.

'I'm kinda confused,' he said. 'What are they doin' here?'

Bonner stepped forward and quickly explained.

'Some of those Lassiter varmints are back there at the marshal's office right now?' he asked when he had finished.

'Yup. That's right. I took a risk. They took a few shots at me.'

'Then what are we waitin' for? Let's go get 'em.'

Tyler stretched out a restraining hand.

'Whoa!' he said. 'I can understand your desire to

get even, but now's not the time. There are other people there. If you go bustin' in some innocent bystanders are likely to get hurt. Besides, those are just a few of them. If you want to really get even, then you'll listen to me and do as I tell you.'

Bonner didn't look convinced and his two companions were quite obviously straining at the bit.

'He's right,' Sadie said. 'Listen to what he says.'

As quickly as he could, Tyler tried to explain the larger situation.

'That's why we don't want to let ourselves get carried away here,' he said. 'After all, we aren't a lynch mob. Just play it cool. If things work out, we'll have the whole Lassiter gang brought to justice.'

'So what are you sayin'?' Bonner asked.

'I'm a saying that right now we get away from here. Most of those outlaws are nowhere near town. They're up in the hills. We know where they are. Once we link up with Freeman and Diamondback, we can make our plans to round 'em up calmly and sensibly. We'll need to be clever because there's still a lot more of them than there are of us. Do you catch my drift?'

Bonner stroked his chin.

'I guess so,' he replied.

'I can see you're all ready to ride. Sadie too.'

Sadie turned to him.

'Is it safe? We might draw attention to ourselves now.'

'I don't think those varmints are going to spend

120

any time looking for me. If they do, they'll be lookin' in the wrong direction. If we don't make any noise we'll be fine.'

'You know where Freeman is?' she said.

'Yup. The only trouble is, I'm pretty sure the Lassiters know where he is too.'

He looked at the men from the Bar 8 and despite the gravity of the situation, he couldn't help a chuckle.

'What's so funny?' Bonner asked.

'Nothin' really. I was just thinkin' of Freeman and old Diamondback. Hell, are they gonna get a surprise when we all come riding in.'

A cold wind blew down from the hills. Thunderheads were gathering and a storm was on its way. The mood of the weather was matched by that of Mort Lassiter as he sat with his brother and the deputy marshal in the squalor of his cabin.

'You've let me down badly, Brinkley,' Lassiter said. There was an icy tone in his voice and his gaze was fixed not on Brinkley but vaguely on the air.

'I did my best,' Brinkley said. 'I did exactly what you told me.'

'You let him get away. You let a woman beat you.'

'How was I to know . . . there was no reason . . . she hit me from behind.'

'I thought I could rely on you.'

'You can rely on me. Look at all the things I've done for you. I've not let you down.'

'You've let us all down now.'

There was a pause. Only Brinkley's heavy breathing disturbed the silence. Outside, the first drops of rain began to fall.

'What do you say, Jute?' Lassiter asked his brother.

'Like you say, he let us down. He let that varmint Tyler get away.'

'It wasn't my fault. I was bushwhacked. I was looking out for Jute when. . . .'

'That's just it. You shouldn't have been lookin' out for Jute. You know what your orders were. You were to stay put till Jute contacted you and keep an eye on Tyler. That shouldn't have been too hard to do considerin' you already had him locked up.'

'I did that part. That was something, wasn't it? I had him in jail. I know I shouldn't have left the place unguarded. It was just that. . . .'

Suddenly Lassiter snapped. The face he turned towards Brinkley was one grotesque snarl as he reached for his gun and stuck it in Brinkley's face.

'I told you where Freeman is. Surely that's something.'

'You only told us what Jute had already found out for himself.'

Brinkley was shaking. Frantically he tried to think of anything that might serve to save his skin. Suddenly he had an inspiration.

'Listen,' he pleaded. 'I think I've got another piece of information.'

'Yeah? What's that? And it had better be good.'

'If I tell you. . . .'

Before he could go any further Lassiter smashed the gun into his face. Blood began to flow freely from his cheek.

'No ifs or buts. You're in no position to make any demands. Just say what you've got to say.'

'I've seen Freeman ride out to an old cabin. He's done it a few times. I only know what you've told me, but I figure if there's any loot involved, that's where he's hidden it.'

The two brothers exchanged glances.

'Where is this place?' Jute asked.

'It's hard to describe. It's a difficult place to find but I can take you there.'

Lassiter turned back to Jute.

'What do you reckon? You think there could be something to it?'

Jute thought for a moment.

'You'd better not be lying,' he said to Brinkley. 'You'd better not be makin' this up to try and save your skin.'

'I promise. It's true. Just give me a chance and I'll show you. We could go now if you want.'

As if in response to his words, from close by there came a clap of thunder.

'Now ain't the right time,' Lassiter snarled. He stared hard at Brinkley for a moment before replacing his gun in its holster.

'You'd better be right about this,' he said, 'because if you're not, I'm gonna have you for a hog-roast.'

Brinkley licked his lips.

'Just give me a chance,' he begged.

Lassiter leaned back against his chair and ran the back of his hand across his chin.

'I should kill you right here and now,' he snarled.

'Please! I won't let you down again.' Lassiter didn't reply. He sat still, allowing the moments to drag by. Finally, he turned to his brother.

'Get him out of my sight. And when you've done that, let the boys know that we'll be ridin' out real soon.'

'You mean we're finally goin' to hit Freeman?'

'Yeah, and I'm pretty sure that we'll catch Tyler at the same time.'

Jute let out a yell.

'Man, that's real good news,' he said. 'To tell you the truth, brother, I've been getting' mighty tired of this whole shebang. You ain't had to hang about that dead-end town like I have. How about we tear the whole thing apart once we've dealt with Freeman and got ourselves the loot?'

Lassiter broke into an ugly laugh.

'That sounds like a real good idea to me,' he said.

Jute let out another whoop.

'Hell, the Lassiter boys are back in business.'

From within the shelter of the overturned steam boat, Tyler and Freeman watched the rain as it slanted down.

'Lucky the storm took its time to break,' Freeman

said. 'If it had started earlier, you might never have got across the river.'

'I'd say I've been ridin' my luck just recently,' Tyler replied.

'How do you mean?'

'Well, if Sadie Roundtree hadn't turned up when she did. . . .' He let the words trail away.

'That dirty skunk Brinkley,' Freeman commented. 'Just wait till I get my hands on him.'

'You might not have to wait too long for that. Unless he gets his hands on you first.'

'I guess it's kinda lucky we've got those Bar 8 boys along,' Freeman mused. 'If it comes to a showdown, they're sure gonna strengthen our hand.'

Tyler glanced at him.

'*If*,' he repeated. 'There's no *if* about it. The way things have panned out, it's just a question of when.'

'I don't feel too happy about havin' Sadie Roundtree involved,' Freeman said. 'When this whole thing explodes, it's gonna be no situation for a woman.'

'I wouldn't let that worry you none. The way she rode into that river . . . I wouldn't like to be the one to try and dissuade her from stickin' around.'

'She sure made herself comfortable in that old cabin, considerin' it ain't exactly on an even keel.'

Tyler gave a muffled laugh, which was interrupted by some grunts from the shadows behind them where the Bar 8 boys lay sleeping. He put his hand to his mouth.

'Don't want to wake anyone,' he said.

'I figure we'd best turn in ourselves,' Freeman responded. 'We can decide on what we do next tomorrow.'

'Yup. It might be an idea to sleep on it. Right now I'm too darn tuckered to be thinkin' properly.'

Without moving from the spot, they lay down and wrapped themselves in their blankets. For a short while Tyler listened to the rain drumming before his eyes closed and he slept.

The storm raged all the next day and most of the day after. Towards evening, taking advantage of a slight break in the weather, Tyler and Freeman made their way to the ford. The normally turbid river was a torrent. It swept by, brown and crested with foam, carrying with it huge logs and invading the beach so that the trunks of the trees higher up the shore were standing deep in the flood water.

'Ain't seen nothin' like it in a long time,' Freeman commented.

'Not much question of crossin' that,' Tyler replied.

'I guess it was weather like this drove the boat ashore in the first place,' Freeman said.

Tyler raised his eyes to the lowering skies.

'How long do you think it will take?' he asked.

'Till we can get over? It's hard to say. Depends on how bad it is in those hills.'

'I guess it can't be much fun for Lassiter and his gang up there.'

'Nope, and that's one reason why I figure they'll

be headin' this way just as soon as they can.'

'You think they know where we are?'

'Don't you? I'm pretty sure they must have figured it out by now.'

Tyler pondered his words for a moment.

'Still, I guess bein' stuck here in this storm is no bad thing,' he said.

'I don't reckon those Bar 8 boys would agree with you. They're gettin' mighty restless. Bonner was tellin' me they were havin' second thoughts about leavin' the herd.'

'What did you say?'

'I told him that he was doin' the right thing. Lassiter can't be allowed to go unpunished. It's the same with all these varmints. Let them get away with it once and they'll do it again.'

Tyler laughed.

'Take it easy,' he said. 'You don't have to persuade me.'

Freeman's face was grim but in a few moments he broke into a grin.

'I guess maybe I'm startin' to get a mite restless too,' he quipped.

'Leastways it's done Miss Roundtree a bit of good. She's been through a hard time lately.'

Freeman thought for a moment.

'I wonder what the marshal's doin'? She said he'd been called away on business.'

'If he's sensible, he'll stay right where he is till all this blows over.'

127

Freeman glanced at Tyler.

'The weather I mean,' Tyler added.

They stood awhile, watching the surging waters before eventually making their way back to the boat.

Marshal Dick had taken advantage of the same lull in the weather to start back for Green Fork. It didn't take long for him to realize he had made a mistake. Fresh banks of cloud scudded across the sky, blown by a chilling wind which quickly gained in strength. The rain, which had dwindled, began to pour down again. He pulled his hat low over his eyes and hunched into his slicker. All around the prairie grass waved and danced so that there seemed to be nothing firm or solid, and the rushing wail of the wind grew louder until it reverberated in his ears like a drum. Bursts of thunder began to roll across the sky as forked lightning snaked and streaked across it with lurid, vivid slashes of light. Suddenly the air was filled with a white fury and his horse reared as hailstones sliced through the storm-driven air.

'Easy, girl,' he said, but his words were lost on the wind.

Some of the stones were as large as a walnut, but though the hailstones soon thinned, he began to look around for somewhere to shelter. He crested a rise and thought he saw what he was looking for. Through the murk and the mist and the driving rain, he saw in the distance what appeared to be a cabin. Changing direction slightly, he began to ride towards it. It was only as he got closer that he saw a number of horses tethered outside, huddled against the storm. He didn't think anything of it. His only feeling was one of relief. If there were horses, it meant that the cabin wasn't deserted, as at first he had presumed, but that there were people who might offer him shelter. The appearance of the cabin certainly supported his initial presumption. It was rickety and down at heel. At any other time he might have taken warning, but he was cold and wet and his main concern was for his horse. He came up to the cabin and swung down from the saddle. As he did so, the door of the cabin was flung open and two men appeared. With a feeling of relief he took a step towards them, but he didn't get any further. He didn't even notice the guns they held in their hands. Without warning, they both raised them and opened fire. He saw the bright bursts of flame and heard the booming echo of their report, but those were the last things he saw or heard as he plunged down into an abyss of pain and night. Standing on the tumbledown veranda of Freeman's old cabin, Lassiter let out a roar of laughter.

'Go and see who it is,' he said.

His companion stepped down into the mud, approached the inert body of the marshal, and peered down into his upturned face upon which the rain was pouring.

'It ain't Freeman, is it?' the voice called. 'Or Tyler?'

'Nope,' the man replied. 'It ain't anybody I've seen before.'

He bent down and looked a little closer.

'He's wearin' a star,' he shouted.

Again Lassiter burst into laughter.

'It must be the marshal. That's a start,' he said. 'That's a first instalment for all the time they locked us away.'

The other man stood upright and returned to the veranda.

'This is gonna be good,' he said. 'I wonder what Brinkley will make of this.'

Lassiter seemed to consider his words for a moment before coming to a decision.

'Brinkley has served his purpose,' he replied. 'As far as I'm concerned, he can go the same way as the marshal.'

The man's eyes gleamed as his hand reached for his six-gun.

'Let me do it,' he said.

Lassiter chuckled grimly.

'All in good time.' He seemed to consider for a moment before continuing. 'But right now I figure we ought to take advantage of the weather and head for that island.'

'What about the loot?'

'We could spend a lot of time lookin' for it. It would be a lot easier if we just let Freeman show us where it is.'

'What if he refuses to do that?'

Lassiter let out a long loud laugh.

'He ain't gonna be in no condition to refuse any-thing,' he said. 'Hell, ain't that what this is all about? By the time we've finished with Freeman, he's gonna wish he'd never tangled with the Lassiter gang.'

The other man joined in the laughter.

'That's why you're the boss,' he chortled.

'Yeah, I'm the boss, and I say let's go get Freeman right now.'

His companion let out a wild whoop.

'Yahoo! We're comin' to getcha, Freeman!'

CHAPTER SEVEN

On the third day since their arrival back on the island, Tyler awakened early. Something had happened to break his sleep and he lay for a few moments wondering what it was. Then he realized that it was silence. The drumming of the rain on the shell of the boat and the whistling of the wind had ceased. He struggled out of his sleeping bag, drew on his trousers and shirt, and stepped outside. The day had dawned, fresh and clear. Early as it was, he wasn't the first to be up and about; Sadie Roundtree had preceded him. She already had a fire going and coffee on the boil.

'Hello,' she said. She looked around and held out her arms.

'Fine day. Makes quite a change, don't it?'

'Yeah. Sure does. You're an early bird.'

'I couldn't sleep. Besides, I was getting to feel kind of cramped up in that old boat. It feels real good to be outside in the open again. Want some coffee?'

'Can't think of anythin' I'd rather have.'

She poured the thick black liquid into two tin mugs and offered him one of them.

'It won't be long till the others start stirring,' she said. 'It's nice to have a bit of time to oneself.'

'Hope I'm not disturbin' you.'

She glanced at him and smiled.

'Of course not. I didn't intend it that way.'

'I know what you mean. Some folks get kind of lonesome when they're out on the trail. Not me. I get restless if there are people around. Old Freeman had the right idea choosing to set himself up out here on the island. If it was me, I wouldn't bother goin' back to Green Fork.'

'What will you do?'

'When this is all over?'

'Yes.' He shrugged.

'Move on again, I guess.'

They fell silent. Glancing around, Tyler could see plenty of evidence of the storm. Several trees had blown over and scattered branches littered the soggy ground. The river had overflowed its banks and was edging around the old hulk. When he looked up, it seemed to be hovering a little lower over his head. His thoughts were interrupted when the others began to appear and soon they were enjoying breakfast.

It was mid-afternoon when Mort Lassiter and his gang approached the river, a little way upstream of the island. The roar of the torrent was loud in their ears as it went swirling by.

'Maybe we should have waited for the floodwater to go down,' Jute said.

'We've waited long enough,' Mort replied. 'I'm tired of waitin'. Aren't you?'

'Yeah, of course I am. I want to get my hands on that low-down coyote just as much as you. But—'

'No buts. This way, with the river like it is, nobody would be expectin' us.'

'It looks mighty rough.'

'What are you worryin' about? Hell, we've swum cattle in worse than this. Remember that time on the Red River?'

Jute grinned.

'Sure. I guess you're right.'

'Of course I'm right. Now go and fetch Brinkley. I need to have a word with him.'

In a few moments Brinkley was brought forward.

'You say we can get to the island. That river looks mighty swollen to me,' Lassiter said.

'It won't be easy, but there's a ford.'

'Remember what happened to the marshal. If you're not tellin' me like it is. . . .'

Lassiter allowed his words to trail away.

'You can trust me,' Brinkley said. 'I know where the ford is.' He glanced towards the foaming torrent.

'Of course I can't be completely sure it's passable.'

'It had better be,' Jute put in.

Mort raised himself in the stirrups to address his men.

'Stay back of the trees,' he said. 'The river should cover any noise we make, but there's no need to go advertisin' ourselves.'

With Brinkley now alongside, the Lassiter brothers led the way. Very quickly, they had their first sight of the wrecked riverboat's chimneys looming above them before they caught glimpses of the great stranded hulk itself through the trees. Mort Lassiter rode closer to the riverbank and peered closely at the island, hoping to catch a glimpse of either Tyler or Freeman, but without success. A fleeting worry crossed his mind. What if they weren't there? But he had it on good authority that they were. He dismissed the thought and rode back to take his place at the head of the group.

It didn't take long till they were approaching the end of the island and Lassiter was about to have another conference with Brinkley when the erstwhile deputy marshal, pointing ahead, led them down towards the river.

'This is it,' he said.

Lassiter held up his hand as a signal for them all to stop.

'What is it?' he said.

'The ford. The best spot to enter the water is just there by that little inlet.'

Lassiter observed the eddying swirling river. Perhaps it looked a little smoother but it could be his imagination.

'I don't like the look of it,' he said.

'The river is in flood. Normally—'

'Never mind *normally*. You reckon we can get across?'

'Well, I can't say for sure but—'

'I'm not interested in ifs and buts. I tell you what. We'll put the theory to the test. You tell me this is the place to cross over to the island. OK. I believe you. You can go first and show the way.'

Brinkley's face visibly blanched. He opened his mouth to say something, to make some excuses, but one glance at Mort Lassiter's ugly expression soon convinced him otherwise. Lassiter turned back to his men, who were anxiously regarding the rushing waters.

'Brinkley is going to show us how to do it,' he barked.

He turned to the unfortunate former lawman.

'OK, get goin'.'

For a moment, Brinkley hesitated before applying his spurs to his horse's flanks and descending the short slope to the river's edge. For the last few yards the animal had to wade through floodwater and it was reluctant to enter the current.

Brinkley looked back at Lassiter. He and his brother stood clear, watching him closely, but the rest of the riders were partly concealed by the foliage. As he did so, Mort Lassiter drew his six-gun and waved it at him menacingly. Coaxing his horse, he urged it forward, holding the reins loosely in one hand while gently slapping its neck with the other.

Although the declivity of the riverbed was gentle, the turbid waters quickly came lapping over his boots and up the horse's flanks and he could sense the beast strain against the pull of the current. He advanced further and was beginning to think that maybe the horse's hoofs would touch bottom all the way across when the water suddenly rose higher and the horse was swimming. Now the current really had them in its grip and they were carried with it beyond the point of the island. Brinkley felt panic begin to well up within him but the horse was strong and began to battle against the pull of the floodwaters. It seemed to sense that its chance of security lay in reaching the island and it strained hard as Brinkley held on tight to its mane. Suddenly he felt a change and the animal seemed to rise beneath him. Its feet had found bedrock again and with a supreme effort it gathered all its strength and they began to emerge on the further bank. Once clear of the water, Brinkley slid from the saddle. For a few moments his emotions were purely those of elation and relief, but then he remembered the situation and looked back across the river. Mort Lassiter and his brother had wasted no time and, once satisfied that the ford was viable, had already entered the water. Brinkley watched with anxious attention, fearful that one or the other of their horses would lose its footing or be swept away, but the outlaws made it without mishap. The rest of the gang followed, and it seemed they would all make it safely when suddenly a voice was heard above the roar of the waters.

'Log! Floatin' log!'

Brinkley turned his head. Bearing down on the riders, borne on the crest of a surging wave, was a huge log. A couple of riders had just entered the water and they managed to hold back their mounts but there were another four in midstream and they had no chance of avoiding the danger. The log hit them like a thunderbolt, driving their horses under the water and tossing them into the maelstrom. The cries of the men and the braying of the horses could just be heard above the roar of the torrent before they were silenced forever as the river swept both men and horses indiscriminately away. Brinkley looked up the river. Coming down on the current were more logs which appeared to have caught on some snag because they were revolving slowly and veering sideways as they came near. As they swept by, Mort Lassiter turned to Brinkley.

'You could have got us all killed,' he said.

'It wasn't my fault. There's no way—'

'Never mind,' Lassiter snapped. 'It's the luck of the draw.'

He looked round. Some of his men were still sitting astride their horses and others had dismounted. Most of them were looking with stony faces at what had happened. Brinkley was shaking but they didn't seem to be affected. He realized that they were hard men who had probably seen a lot worse.

'All right, everybody,' Lassiter said. 'Now we're

here, let's get down to business. We've got Freeman and Tyler right where we want them. They can't get off the island. They can't escape us now. So what are we waitin' for? Let's go get them!'

His words drew a response, but it was muted.

'We'll leave the horses here,' Lassiter continued, 'and comb the island on foot.'

With that he dismounted and those still in the saddle did likewise. Once the horses had been tethered, they began to spread out and make their way through the trees.

The morning passed and the sun came out, helping to dry the sodden landscape. Freeman and his guests had been working to repair some of the damage done by the storm when suddenly the silence was shattered by the clap of rifle fire. Instantly Tyler called to the others to get back into the shelter of the wrecked paddle steamer and began running himself. He just managed to fling himself through the door when the first shot was succeeded by a fusillade of fire from several different quarters. Bullets pinged and whined from the metal parts of the hull and thudded into the woodwork. He didn't need to explain what had happened. The others quickly realized that the assault they had been waiting for had finally arrived. They had taken up their various positions and were already returning fire. When he looked out of a window, he could see spurts of flame coming from all directions. They were obviously well outnumbered. They could easily have been taken by surprise so he surmised that someone had seen him and instinctively opened fire. It suggested that Lassiter and his gang were not very well disciplined, which might work to their favour. He had no time for further reflection as, taking aim at a patch of bushes, he began to pump lead. The response was immediate and he quickly pulled back his head as a slug ripped into the hull, showering him with sharp fragments of wood. The clock which had long stopped on the mantelpiece shattered as another bullet ricocheted into the cabin. Tyler levered off another round and was pleased to notice that a couple of bodies lay spreadeagled on the ground outside. Although the shooting was wild and ill-disciplined, they were still accounting for some of the attackers. He glanced round for the others. The three men from the Bar 8 were firing rapidly. Their faces were taut but when one of them turned towards him, his features were creased in a grin. Far from being fazed by being caught by surprise, they seemed to be actually enjoying it. They had been getting restive for some time and Tyler's guess was that they were pleased that the waiting was over. Diamondback was busy reloading. He couldn't see Freeman or Sadie and for a moment he was concerned till he remembered that their stations were in a cabin to the rear of the saloon.

'OK back there?' he yelled.

'We're fine!' Freeman's voice came in reply.

Tyler smiled briefly. Everyone seemed to be

bearing up well. Then, taking advantage of a temporary lull in the firing, he took another look out of the window. There was no sign of anything moving, which wasn't surprising considering the lushness of the vegetation. As he withdrew his head from the opening, a voice cut through the comparative silence.

'Listen up! It's Freeman we want. As for you, Tyler, and anyone else in there, you can go free as far as we're concerned. Just send out Freeman!'

Tyler was thinking quickly. He guessed that the voice was Lassiter's. It was obviously a ruse, and the very fact that Lassiter had chosen to shout his message was an indication that he was somewhat disconcerted by his reception. In particular, he couldn't know how many people he was dealing with. Presumably he had expected Freeman and Tyler, maybe even the oldster, but it was obvious to him now that they weren't the only two involved. It gave him encouragement but he was worried at the same time that Freeman might do something cavalier in response. Although he, too, must be aware that Lassiter was not to be trusted, he was quite likely to make a gesture and offer himself for the sake of the others. Before he could respond, Tyler himself called out.

'Go to hell, Lassiter! We knew you were comin' and we're ready!'

A few moments passed. Tyler exchanged glances once more with the Bar 8 men before Lassiter's voice

141

rang out again.

'Just send out Freeman and the rest of you can go free!'

'No deal, Lassiter!'

'Don't be stupid. You haven't got a chance. We've got the place surrounded. All we want is Freeman.'

The Bar 8 men grinned once more.

'We've sure got them rattled,' Bonner said. 'I don't think this is just how your friend Lassiter figured it.'

Tyler turned back to the window.

'If you want Freeman, you'd better come and get him. We're waitin' for you.'

He didn't feel quite so confident as he tried to sound. In truth, their situation was perilous, but at least Lassiter couldn't be sure of how small they were in number.

'I'll give you ten minutes. Send out Freeman or you're dead!'

Silence descended again. In a few seconds Freeman and Sadie appeared in the doorway.

'Maybe I should go,' Freeman said.

'Don't be stupid. Lassiter's just stallin' for time.'

'We're all in this together,' Sadie said, taking Freeman's arm.

Before anyone could say anything further, there suddenly came a sound like the loud splintering of wood. The room seemed to sway and some of the furniture crashed to the floor. The light fittings were swinging in a crazy fashion and then with a juddering creak and shudder, the ship lurched to one side, throwing everyone on their knees. Clutching at anything in order to gain purchase, they got to their feet again. The boat had settled but the creaking sounds continued.

'Hell, what was that?' Diamondback muttered.

'Must be the storm. All that water – I guess the old girl was never too steady to start with.'

'We need to get out of here,' Tyler replied.

Freeman was plunged in thought for a few moments before saying anything.

'Listen,' he said. 'I've got a plan. Lassiter and his gang are all out there on the forest side of the boat. It's unlikely any of them have got round to the point of the island. Why would they? If we climb up through the boat, we can make our escape through one of the portholes. At the very least, we wouldn't be any worse off than we are now.'

The others considered his words.

'I don't like bein' bottled up here anyway,' Tyler said. 'It's not how we figured it. Let's do as Freeman suggests.'

As if adding to the debate, the boat let out a loud groan and sank slightly further to the starboard.

'All right, follow me,' Freeman said.

He led the way out of the ship's saloon and through the adjoining cabin to an iron staircase in the rear. It had settled into a crazy angle but they were able to climb its damaged rungs. It led them to another staircase and a corridor from which several cabins opened. Their doors swung loosely on their hinges. They entered the nearest one and Tyler peered through its porthole.

'We can get through to the side of the boat. It's on the side away from Lassiter and his gang, but you'll need to be careful. The boat is at a dangerous angle. We'll make our way to the stern and get down via the paddle wheel.'

They looked at one another uneasily.

'Its not easy, but it can be done. I'll lead the way. Just do as I tell you.'

'We haven't got much choice,' Sadie said.

As if in corroboration, a fresh burst of gunfire suddenly erupted from the other side of the boat.

'Looks like Lassiter has lost patience,' Tyler said. 'Come on. Let's go.'

Freeman began to tug at the glass of the porthole, but it was rusted and wouldn't yield.

'Here, let me try,' Bonner said.

He took hold and strained hard, his muscles bulging. Just when it seemed his efforts must fail, the glass swung open.

'It's a bit of a squeeze,' Freeman commented, 'but here goes.'

He took hold of the edge of the porthole and slithered through, feet first. As they touched the hull, he held on firmly while seeking a foothold. When he was satisfied his feet were solidly placed, he let go. He was used to clambering about the hull, but the boat had shifted its position and the angle was steeper than previously. He was still able to move forward. Poking his head though the porthole, he indicated for the others to follow. Diamondback came next without any particular difficulty because he was the smallest, followed by Bonner and his two Bar 8 men. They were on hand to assist Sadie and Tyler brought up the rear.

'Don't look down,' Freeman said. 'Take it slowly and it'll be just like walkin' along Main Street. Might be an idea if we hold on to one another. Are you ready?'

Adjusting his position and leaning to one side, he began to ease his way along the hull. The others followed his example, but quickly Sadie and the Bar 8 men dropped into a more crawling stance, advancing crabwise above the top of the letters painted as if by a giant hand along the side of the boat: *Elenore*. Slowly but surely they reached the stern and the great paddle wheel.

'Looks like this is goin' to be the hard part,' Diamondback said.

The wheel looked huge and threatening. The top of it towered over them and it seemed a long, long way down.

'The way the blades are engineered should make it easier to climb,' Freeman said.

Disregarding Freeman's previous advice, Tyler looked down.

'Maybe we could kinda slither down the side of the boat?' he suggested.

Freeman took a glance.

'You could try it,' he replied. 'But it's steep and there's nothing to stop you if you start sliding.'

Tyler took a second look.

'I figure you're right,' he said. 'The paddle wheel's the better option.'

While they were deliberating, the rattle of gunfire continued.

'Lassiter must be wonderin' why there's no return of fire,' Bonner said.

'You've got a point,' one of the Bar 8 men responded. 'Maybe he thinks he's killed us all.'

'If that's the case, he might try and storm the boat,' Bonner added.

They were considering the matter when Freeman broke in.

'Never mind that,' he said. 'This is no time for speculatin'. We need to concentrate on climbin' down that wheel.'

They were still hesitating when Sadie spoke up.

'I've had a thought. What if we can make our way round to the other side? The way the boat is leaning now, we could maybe jump?'

'I doubt whether we'd be able to cling on,' Tyler replied.

'Wait a minute,' Freeman said. 'There's a rail we could hold on to. It could be worth a try.'

'I don't figure we could manage that wheel,' Bonner said. 'The blades are just too far apart.'

Freeman looked from one to another.

'What do you think then? Should we give Sadie's idea a go?'

There was general assent.

'It'll still be a long drop,' Freeman continued. 'And another thing.'

'Yeah, what's that?'

'We're sheltered from Lassiter and his boys here at the stern. If we make our way round to the side, we'll be getting closer to them.'

'There's plenty of vegetation between them and us. They're under cover. I doubt whether they'd ever see us.'

'Are we agreed? Then let's go. I'll go first again and you follow.'

Freeman began to inch his way round the stern. When the camber began to get really difficult, he edged higher and reached out to hold the bottom of the rail which ran round the back end of the boat. He advanced a little further but soon realized the boat was leaning at such an angle that further progress was beginning to become impossible. He came to a halt and turned to face the others.

'I don't think this is going to work.'

'So what now?'

Suddenly he was struck by another idea.

'The smokestacks,' he said. 'We could crawl along the smokestacks. They reach lower than the tree-tops.'

They exchanged glances.

'I don't think we've got much choice,' Tyler said.

147

'How do we get to them?'

'We'll need to climb over the rail and make our way over the deck.'

Sadie looked up.

'I don't think I can do it,' she said. 'I don't think I can raise myself up.'

'Don't worry. Once a couple of us are over the rail, we can heave you over.'

There was little enthusiasm for the scheme, but Tyler's words struck a chord. They didn't have much choice.

'Here goes then,' said Freeman.

'Hold on,' Bonner said. 'This is going to need some strength. Let me try it.'

Reaching up, he seized hold of the rail and began to haul himself up. As his feet kicked out in an effort to gain purchase against the hull, his two companions attempted to give him such support as they could without dislodging themselves. Bonner put out all his strength to pull himself level with the rails. For a few moments he clung to them, recovering his energy, before with a massive effort he succeeded in climbing over. The two Bar 8 men followed without too much difficulty and once they had made it to the deck, they were able to lean over and haul up first Sadie and then the more diminutive figure of Diamondback. Last of all came Tyler.

'Keep holding tight to the rail,' Freeman commanded.

'Hold on a minute till I get my sea-legs,'

Diamondback replied.

The others were of a similar frame of mind. Their legs were shaking as they braced them against the tilt of the upper deck, and the physical difficulty was accompanied by a feeling of disorientation. The boat was leaning now at a more acute angle even than previously and intermittent loud creaks indicated its perilous condition. Once they had rested and adjusted to their situation, they set off slowly, bracing themselves against the gradient. The sound of gunfire was louder now but as they made their slow and cautious progress it dwindled and then died away. They barely registered the fact, although Tyler for one was praying that Freeman was right when he gave his opinion that the outlaws would not see them through their cover of thick vegetation.

Once they reached the vicinity of the smoke-stacks, they faced another difficulty, which was the problem of how to crawl up the slope of the deck to reach them. They did it on hands and knees, not without moments of anxiety, especially when Sadie slipped at one point and was only arrested in her slide by the firm hold of Bonner beside her. When they had reached the nearest smokestack Freeman didn't waste any time in climbing on to it.

'It's just about wide enough to walk on,' he said, 'but if you've no head for heights, it might be better to carry on crawling.'

He took a few tentative steps forward.

'The angle isn't so bad,' he said. 'I think it'll be a

lot easier than climbing about the hull of the *Elenore*.'

With his arms outspread and treading very carefully, he began to walk. With greater or lesser difficulty, the others hoisted themselves in turn on to the blackened smokestack, following in the same order they had previously, the Bar 8 men following Freeman's example but the others going on all fours. It was fortunate for them all that the wind which had blown furiously at times during the storm had completely abated otherwise they might have been swept from their precarious platform by a sudden gust. What Freeman was concerned about was whether the metal of the smokestack had corroded over the years and he felt gingerly ahead with his foot before taking each step. At the back of the group Tyler suddenly felt a whiff of euphoria similar to the one he had experienced when he had set off in the canoe, and rose to his feet. Planting his feet as firmly as he could, he took a few moments to look around him. It was certainly an exhilarating position to be in. He had a wonderful view of the country all round – the forest with the river running through and beyond that, the land rising to the distant hills. In the clear air he could hear the sound of the rushing waters and, above it, the shrill calling of a bird. Beneath his feet he had the sensation that the smokestack was quivering and humming. For those few moments at least he had no sense of present or future danger, and even when he heard the intrusive sound of a human voice calling something he remained undisturbed. He strained to make out the words but to no avail and then the voice ceased calling as suddenly as it had begun. He looked over to where the outlaws were concealed and after a few moments he saw figures running forward across the narrow stretch of empty space between the trees and the riverboat. He was taken aback and couldn't think for a moment what they were till he realized that it was Lassiter and his men and they were storming the riverboat. The cry must have been Lassiter's final attempt to get Freeman released. The outlaws had obviously concluded that they had overcome any resistance and the place was theirs for the taking. Afraid that he might be spotted, he came back from his reverie. He didn't know if anyone else had seen Lassiter's men but if they hadn't there didn't seem much point in drawing their attention to it for the moment. Instead, he concentrated on his next move and took a few upright steps before sinking back again to his hands and knees.

He was concentrating now on maintaining his hold on the smokestack and it came as a surprise when he found there was no longer air beneath him but the tangled branches of trees. Like those in front, he had to take care to brush aside twigs and leaves. A little further and they all came to a halt. He looked down and could see the ground but it still seemed a long way down.

'Everyone OK?' Freeman's voice was hushed but there was no mistaking a note of hope in it.

'It's getting rather overgrown but I think we can get a bit lower.'

Tyler tried to peer ahead. As he did so the smoke-stack seemed to take a sudden lurch and then sank lower, slicing through the foliage.

'What the. . . .' Diamondback began, but got no further as the smokestack shook and quivered before taking another plunge. They were all holding on grimly but when Tyler took another look down, the ground was a lot closer.

'We can make it,' he called, 'by climbing down the trees.'

For a moment he considered a straight drop, but changed his mind. Reaching out for the nearest branch, he moved from the smokestack into the tree. He had to stretch to reach the next branch down but it wasn't too difficult and, bit by bit, he succeeded in reaching a branch not far above the ground. It was still a fair drop but he didn't waste any time. Lowering himself as far as he could, he let go and plunged to the earth, landing with a shuddering bump. He picked himself up as Bonner landed next to him.

'Come on!' he called. 'Get down now before any-thing else happens.'

The others quickly followed suit, with a greater or lesser degree of assistance. When they were all safely back on the ground they paused, panting from exer-tion, till a loud noise from above made them look up. The smokestack seemed to be swaying.

'Quickly! Let's get out of here before she goes,' Freeman said.

Tyler wasn't sure exactly what Freeman meant, but as they took to their heels it soon became obvious. With an almighty tearing and rending and a noise like a roll of thunder, the smokestack came crashing down as the riverboat overturned. For a frightening moment the hull of the boat overhung them as they raced from beneath its shadow. Like a monstrous leviathan the boat rocked and then settled to its new position, crushing anything beneath it. They continued running till the point of the island came into view when they came to a halt, panting and bemused. Then it began to dawn on them what a narrow escape they'd had and how close they had come to being killed.

'If that boat had overturned even five minutes earlier. . . .'

Diamondback didn't finish his sentence. Together with his companions, he looked back at the vast bulk of the overturned riverboat.

'It must have been the storm,' Freeman said. 'I guess it undermined whatever foundation the boat was resting on.'

They were silent, overcome by the enormity of what had just happened. For the moment none of them were thinking of Lassiter till Tyler recalled what he had seen.

'I don't know if anyone else noticed, but I saw Lassiter and his gang making for the boat.'

They looked at one another.

'If they got too close, they wouldn't have had much of a chance,' Freeman commented.

'I reckon they got close all right. If they weren't crushed beneath it, chances are they died inside it.'

Tyler's words hung in the air, silencing them, before Bonner eventually spoke.

'We'll need to go careful. There might be some of 'em still left alive.'

Again they were silent. Each one of them was trying to come to terms with what had happened. The enormity of the event and the dramatic nature of their escape was almost overwhelming. They were in a state of shock. The silence continued until Tyler suddenly broke into a laugh.

'What's so funny?' Freeman said.

'I'm sorry. Take a look at Diamondback.'

They looked at the oldster. There was something odd about him but for a moment none of them realized what it was. Even Diamondback looked perplexed.

'You've lost your glass eye,' Tyler said. 'It's the one casualty we seem to have sustained.'

His words seemed to break the spell that had fallen on them and, following Tyler's example, they all began to laugh.

'Hell,' Diamondback said, putting his hand up to the empty socket. 'You're right and I didn't even notice.'

*

It didn't take long to confirm the fate of the outlaws. Parts of the interior of the boat were inaccessible, but if there were any survivors they had fled the scene. The bodies Freeman and his companions discovered, they buried. Some of them were disfigured, but one at least was easily identifiable. It was Jute Lassiter, but they couldn't identify the remains of Mort, Jute's brother and the leader of the gang.

'Whether he's dead or alive,' Freeman said, 'it doesn't matter. The Lassiter gang are finished. There's nothing to fear from them now.'

When the grisly job was done, they spent that night and part of the next day before leaving the island, partly to allow time for the waters to subside. They considered taking the outlaws' horses but decided to leave them behind and round them up on another occasion. They crossed in safety and set their course first for the tumbledown shack which Freeman had once considered home and now held the secret of the loot the Lassiters had been looking for.

As they approached it seemed to Freeman that it looked even more decrepit than he remembered it. There was litter in the tangled grass and mud of what had once been the yard.

'Someone's been here,' he said.

Instantly they were on the alert. Bringing their horses to a halt, they watched and listened closely.

'I figure if anyone's been, they've left now,' Tyler said eventually.

They continued their observations. They were

about convinced that Tyler was right when Sadie held up her hand.

'What was that?' she said.

The others turned to her.

'I thought I heard something. Listen!'

For a time they could hear nothing and then, very faintly, they detected a sound like a distant moan.

'It seemed to come from over by those bushes,' Diamondback said.

'You wait here,' Freeman said. 'I'll go take a look.'

'Be careful,' Bonner said.

Freeman dismounted, drew his gun, and moved carefully towards the bushes. He was still a little distance away when he came to a halt. He peered more closely.

'What is it?' Tyler called.

'There's someone lying there.'

The others began to dismount as Freeman moved on again. Suddenly he sheathed his gun and broke into a run. He reached the bushes, parted them and got down on one knee.

'It's Marshal Dick!' he shouted.

Instantly Sadie sprang forward, followed by the others. In a moment she was at the marshal's side.

'What's happened to him?' she asked.

Freeman felt awkward. He could see her pain and anguish but he had no choice.

'He's been shot. Twice,' he replied.

'He's still alive,' she said. 'Quick, we've got to do something.'

'Let's get him inside,' Freeman said.

As carefully as possible, the men from the Bar 8 lifted the wounded marshal and carried him into the building. Tyler got his bedroll and they laid him on it.

'He's in a bad way,' Freeman said.

'I wonder how long he's been lyin' there.'

'We've got to get help. He needs a doctor.'

With those words Freeman made for the door. Tyler followed him and in a matter of seconds they were back in the saddle and heading for town. They rode hard, knowing that if there was any chance of the marshal surviving, they couldn't waste a second of time. It wasn't far. Soon they were clattering down Main Street. They pulled up outside the marshal's office and tied their horses to the hitch-rail. The doctor's shingle hung just a little way further down, but when they arrived the doctor wasn't there.

'He's probably out visitin',' Tyler said. 'If we split up we'll have a better chance of findin' him.'

'Sounds sensible, but let's try the saloon first. I know the doc and he ain't averse to takin' a drink between his rounds. If he's not there, someone might know where to find him.'

They moved quickly to the Spur Saloon and stepped through the batwings. The atmosphere was hazy with smoke but as they approached the bar there was no mistaking the three men who stood hunched over the counter. It was Lassiter with Brinkley and two of his henchmen. Freeman and

157

Tyler exchanged glances. They were of one mind.

'Lassiter!' Freeman barked.

The gang leader swung round. For a moment his features registered surprise and then, when he recognized Freeman, they creased into an ugly snarl.

'So you're still here,' he rasped.

'Still here,' Freeman replied. He turned to Brinkley. 'Shouldn't you be takin' these men in? Nope, I guess not. You're sure not makin' any pretence to be deputy marshal now, are you?'

Brinkley's lip was trembling. He looked with fear and surprise at Freeman and Tyler. The other two gunmen began to fan out as the scraping of chairs indicated that the rest of the clientele were seeking to get as far out of the way as possible. Suddenly Tyler had a moment of inspiration.

'It was you who shot Marshal Dick, wasn't it?' he said.

Lassiter's response was to reach for his guns. Quick as he was, Freeman was quicker. As Lassiter's hand closed on the trigger, Freeman's .44 spat lead and the outlaw spun backwards as his shot missed its target and buried itself in the ceiling. Tyler had the two outlaws covered and as they opened fire, he ducked low and fanned the hammer of his revolver. A spatter of bullets caught the two full in the chest and swept them clean off their feet. Freeman fired again and Lassiter's gun fell from his hand. For a few moments he stood still, blood frothing from his mouth, before he fell forwards, hitting the floor with a terrific crash. Freeman swung his gun towards Brinkley but the ex-deputy marshal was stood immobile, frozen with fright. After the roar of the guns the saloon seemed unnaturally quiet but presently a buzz of voices began to resume. The bartender came round from behind his counter and examined the bodies. Looking up, he shook his head.

'Dead,' he said. 'Someone go get the undertaker.'

Brinkley was sobbing. The bartender went up to him. Blood was trickling down Brinkley's arm.

'Looks like a flesh wound. Maybe it was a ricochet. Get the doc as well.'

Freeman and Tyler re-holstered their guns.

'Yeah,' Freeman said. 'Bring the doc as well.'

They turned and strode back through the batwings to await his arrival. As they stood on the boardwalk, Freeman turned to Tyler.

'Thanks,' he said.

The figure of the doc appeared rounding a corner.

'It doesn't matter what it takes to fix the marshal and get him back in business,' Freeman said. 'The loot those varmints were lookin' for don't amount to anythin' like they imagined, but it'll pay for his treatment.'

He paused.

'And the rest is yours if you care to stick around.'